BOSSY
BRT

New York Times & USA Today Bestselling Author
KENDALL RYAN

Bossy Brit

Copyright © 2019 Kendall Ryan

Content Editing by Elaine York

Proofreading by Virginia Tesi Carey

Cover Design and Formatting by Uplifting Author
Services

About the Book

Sexy billionaire Liam Bennett is cocky, dangerously handsome, and more importantly, my new boss. If only my ovaries didn't flutter when he was near—yeah, that'd be super helpful.

When our long hours lead to a dare—and an X-rated encounter—I never expected it to be the hottest sex of my life.

It'd also be super helpful if Liam didn't know it and taunt me about it every chance he got. Unable to deny our attraction any longer, our work relationship brings a whole new meaning to the term *inbox*.

But being with him comes with some baggage—like an ex-wife and three kids kind of baggage. And a lawyer who wants half of his company.

Unsure that I'm cut out for this new level of complicated, my traitorous ovaries beg me to try.

Heaven help us all.

CHAPTER ONE

Noelle

"**N**oelle? Hello?" a deep voice rumbles my name, and I almost jump out of my seat.

Around the long conference table, all eyes in the room swing over to me. I'm supposed to be taking notes on the business meeting I'm in, but I'd been doing what I usually do at work: ogling my way-too-sexy boss, Liam.

I drag my eyes up his broad chest and blink twice. "I'm sorry, what was that?" I clear my throat, trying to hide my embarrassment. But I'm pretty sure my mouth was just hanging open. I was having a particularly vivid fantasy about him taking me into his office, pushing me up against the wall and ripping my dress off while he whispered filthy endearments in that wonderfully naughty British accent of his.

Although I don't stress about climbing the career ladder, I'm still a hard worker and would never allow myself to drift off during an important meeting. But at any other job, my boss wouldn't be six-foot-two inches with thick, dark hair, piercing green eyes and a British accent that makes my knees weak. He's basically the definition of man candy, and I'm dying to try a piece. Or ten.

"Do you have those files I asked you to make copies of?" Liam asks sternly, giving me a look like we're going to have a long discussion about my negligence later. This isn't the first time I've been caught daydreaming. In fact, it's something I do way too much of whenever he's within a five-hundred-foot radius.

I nod and rise to my feet to begin passing out the files to each member of his executive team, hoping I'm not blushing as much as I think I am. I know Liam isn't going to be happy about this, but if he wants me to focus, maybe he shouldn't sit across from me looking like he was just named sexiest man alive by *People* magazine.

Plus, today he's wearing that cologne I love, the one that makes me have a mini orgasm every time he comes anywhere near me. Not that he needs cologne to turn me on. His sculpted chest and trim waist, accentuated by those designer power suits he wears every day does the trick all on its own.

I started working as the assistant to Liam Bennett, the CEO of Griffin Real Estate Investments, a few months ago. It's by no means my dream job, but it pays the bills and allows me the free time to do the things I really love to do outside of work. The only downside is that the boss is serious, demanding, and an absolute panty dropper. Oh, and if you couldn't already guess, totally off limits. Apparently, it's unprofessional to sleep with your boss. Who knew?

It's probably not a great idea to fantasize about him, either, but that doesn't stop me from imagining what it would be like to sneak into his office late one night and ride him like the stud he is.

Thankfully, the meeting ends without another incident. I'm hoping I can sneak back to my desk unnoticed, but Liam clears his throat loudly before I get out the door.

"Noelle, my office," he snaps as everyone begins filing past me. Usually I'd hate to have a boss order me around the way he does, but with Liam it just turns me on more. Between the power suits and that demanding attitude, I spend what feels like the majority of my day drooling over him. In fact, it's amazing I can even get work done. But despite Liam's alluring presence and constant demands, he seems surprisingly pleased with my work so far.

"Care to explain what happened back there?" Liam asks angrily as I step into his office. I shut the door so the whole office doesn't have to hear me get chewed out. *Wouldn't you like to know?* I think, then mentally slap myself. *Not the time to get sassy, Noelle.*

"I bring you in on those meetings to help me, not so you can daydream," he continues as he takes a seat behind his desk. He has the corner office, with floor-to-ceiling glass windows, amazing views, and a huge, mahogany desk.

His forest green eyes are watching me intently, and his full lips are turned down at the corners. Even angry, he still makes me want to crawl across his desk and see how fast I can rip that Calvin Klein suit off of him. If he bosses me around this much in real life, I can only imagine the way he'd boss me around in the bedroom. The thought alone makes my stomach flip, and I feel my nipples harden beneath my dress. I hold my notepad and pen against my chest, hoping Liam doesn't notice.

I take a seat in from of him and clear my throat, resting my eyes a few inches to Liam's left. It's a lot easier to concentrate when I'm not staring at his chiseled jaw and lose-yourself-in-them green eyes.

"I'm sorry I was a little out of it today," I begin, but my phone buzzes against the hard, wooden surface of his desk before I can continue. *Shit.* I thought I'd put it on silent.

"Jesus, Noelle, seriously?" Liam says, as my phone continues to buzz and light up like a freaking slot machine in Vegas. "What could be so important that you need your phone on right now?" His eyes drift down to the screen.

"I apologize, I thought it was off," I say, reaching forward to silence my phone, but before I get to it, I pause with horror. It's my friends, Jess and Maxine, messaging me in our group chat. To make matters worse, they happen to be messaging me about how I should "bang" my "totally hot boss." It takes me a second to recover, but I grab my phone and turn it on silent. From the look on Liam's face, though, it's obvious he's seen everything.

"I'm so sorry," I say, in full blush now. "Those are my friends, and it's just an inside joke. They're totally kidding," I stammer, but it's too late. I'm not only terrible at lying, but my tendency to blush easily gives me away every time. There's a smile playing across Liam's lips, and I know he doesn't believe my terrible excuse for a second.

"An inside joke about banging your hot boss?" He smirks, leaning back in his chair. I can tell he's suppressing a laugh. Even in my mortification I can't help but notice the way his biceps strain against the fabric of his suit.

"Yeah, it's a long story," I say, frantically grabbing my things from his desk. I almost trip on the leg of the chair in my rush to stand up. "Sorry about that. And about earlier, it won't happen again."

I walk out of his office as quickly as I can, throw my things down on my desk, and practically run to the ladies' room. I lock myself in a stall and put my face in my hands, letting out a sigh. I debate how long I can get away with hiding in the restroom, then consider sneaking out a back window before I remember we're on the twenty-fifth floor. The idea of plummeting to my death is only slightly more terrifying than the idea of facing Liam again, but I know I have to leave the bathroom sometime.

As I walk past Liam's office to get back to my desk, I purposely avoid looking at him, but I can feel his eyes on me. I start work again, trying not to think about the little slip-up and what I might have just gotten myself into.

"So, he knows you want to bang him, so what?" Maxine says, taking a long sip of her dirty martini. "This is a good thing."

"I'm sorry, how is it a good thing?" I ask, downing my second margarita. After my little mishap, I texted my group chat with Jess and Maxine telling them that we needed to meet for emergency drinks after work. After I filled them in on what happened, I expected them to share my mortification and tell me I needed to stop imagining how my new boss looks naked and focus on keeping this job. Instead, they seem excited that he saw our little text conversation.

"Now that he knows, you can make a move and finally get some of that high-powered, CEO di--," Maxine starts, but Jess cuts her off.

"I think what Maxine is *trying* to say is that now that your attraction is out in the open, you don't have to deal with all of that sexual tension anymore," Jess says, tucking a strand of her short brown hair behind her ear.

I stare back and forth between them. I invited them for drinks to make me feel better, not to encourage me to do the crazy thing I've been trying to stop myself from doing.

"You want me to sleep with him?" I ask, mouth agape. I can feel my anxiety skyrocketing. "I was thinking something more along the lines of changing my name and moving to Mexico, so I never have to face him again, but sure, let's exacerbate the situation even more with your plan."

"We're both Team Bang Your Boss." Maxine grins, crossing her arms. "Stop being such a prude and just jump him already."

I look back and forth between them. They're both grinning at me and I can't help but laugh.

"Jess, I expected better from you," I say, raising an eyebrow at her.

Maxine opens her mouth in mock offense, tossing back her long blonde hair. "What is that supposed to mean?"

"I think she's referring to the fact that you slept with your last two bosses," Jess reminds her, grinning.

"Yeah, and it was some of the best sex I've

ever had. There's nothing like forbidden sex, the paycheck was just the icing on the cake." Maxine winks, finishing her drink. "I have no regrets."

"Can we get another round?" I ask the server. "I'm way too sober for this."

Jess and Maxine are watching me intently, and I realize they're loving my drama a little too much.

"You guys, I'm too old for this. I could maybe justify it if we were younger, but I'm turning thirty this year. Shouldn't I be making rational, mature decisions about who I sleep with?"

"Fuck it." Maxine waves away my concerns. "You only live once, and you don't even care about this job that much. If all you get out of it are a few good paychecks and some hot sex before you get caught, I'd say you got a pretty good deal."

I look to Jess. Normally, she's the levelheaded one who can counter Maxine's overly carefree attitude. I'm hoping she'll encourage me to stay away from Liam, but she just shrugs.

"Honestly, I agree with her. It's not like this is your dream job or anything, and if he's as hot as you say he is, it might be worth it to just throw caution to the wind."

Maxine high fives Jess and they both turn to grin at me.

"I can't believe this," I say, taking my margarita from our server. "So, you two actually think I should sleep with my boss?"

"It's just a little harmless fun." Maxine smirks. "And if it goes south after you or he goes south, if you catch my drift, then you can both be professional about it, or you can just quit. No harm done."

I can't help but laugh at the situation I find myself in.

Even though I'll still be slightly mortified to see Liam at work tomorrow, I'm starting to feel better about the whole thing. Or maybe it's just the third margarita kicking in.

"Wait! What if he rejects me?" The thought comes out of my mouth before I have a chance to process it. I'd been so focused on the fact that he's my boss and how taboo that is that I hadn't even thought about that aspect of things.

"You said he was smiling after he read the texts," Maxine says, raising an eyebrow at me. "*And* he teased you about it. I mean, come on, this guy has a total boner for you."

"Besides, have you looked at yourself? Of course, he's into you." Jess smiles at me.

"Come on, just do it. Work hard, play harder, right?" Maxine says with a wink, and I snort into my drink.

As much as I love them for being so encouraging, there is no way. As I walk home, I try to remind myself of all the downsides of my workplace attraction. The trouble is, when I picture Liam's green eyes staring into mine, all of the doubts melt away and I can only think about how much I want his hands on me. I don't know if it's the margaritas, my friends, or the thought of Liam, but the more I think about it the more the little, rational voice inside my head is fading away, and the thought of sleeping with my boss is starting to actually seem like a good idea.

CHAPTER TWO

Liam

I've always been a man who knows what he wants and goes after it. It's how I met and married my wife. It's how we had three kids while both working full-time. And it's how I worked my way up the corporate ladder and became the youngest CEO in the history of Griffin Real Estate Investments at the age of thirty-five.

But now, I'm on the other side of a long divorce, forced to share custody of my kids with a bitter ex-wife who makes Godzilla seem like a playful kitten, and I've got a new assistant who's such a knockout I can hardly get through a workday without imagining her taking a ride on my cock—which is seriously distracting me from running this multimillion-dollar company.

"I'm just saying, you could stand to relax a little bit," Jamie, my chief strategist says, interrupting my thoughts. He's been trying to convince me for the past fifteen minutes to go on a date with a woman he knows from the gym. I've been zoning out, sick of hearing the same thing from him. The problem with Jamie is he's not a coworker, but my best friend, and he's way too concerned about my personal life when he should be focusing on his own work. He's been on my ass about letting loose and taking a break pretty much since we met, and it's gotten even worse since my divorce.

"CEOs don't relax, Jamie. That's how they became CEOs."

Jamie sighs and sits back in his chair, his hands behind his head, like he's heard it all before. Which he has, for the past seventeen years. We went to college together, and sometimes I think Jamie wants me to be the same guy who stayed out all night and always won the keg stand contest. But I'm just not. I grew up. And I have mountains of responsibility that keep me in check.

"Just go out with her once. Maybe you'll even get laid. It's been how long again?" He smirks at me, and I shake my head. It *has* been awhile. Longer than I'd care to admit, in fact, but my nasty divorce made the idea of pursuing a new relationship sound more exhausting than it's worth.

"I'm too old to go on a blind date. And I'm definitely too old for a one-night stand. I have kids, remember?" I tell him, hoping this will make him drop the subject.

I specifically haven't told him about what I saw on Noelle's phone yesterday, or about my very in-convenient attraction to her. Partly because I don't want to give him any ammunition to encourage me to pursue my assistant, and partly because I want to keep this between me and Noelle.

The truth is, every time I catch her staring at me with that look on her face like she's picturing all the things she wants me to do to her, I feel things behind my zipper that I haven't felt in years. Or maybe ever. Even when things were good with my ex, they were never as steamy as I've felt just standing next to Noelle. I'm not the kind of man who gets easily distracted by anything, especially when it could affect work. And I'm nowhere near the kind of creep who would hit on his assistant. But no one in business school told me how to deal with my assistant coming onto *me*. Especially not one with full lips, perky tits and legs for days, that I keep imagining clamped around my waist. Which is exactly what's been happening ever since I hired Noelle St. James.

My computer pings, pulling me out of my thoughts. Probably for the best, considering that when I think about Noelle for too long I start to feel an ache in my groin that makes it impossible to work.

"Shit," I say, setting down my cup of coffee. I look up at Jamie. "Looks like it's going to be another late night at the office."

"What happened?" Jamie asks, surprised. "I thought everything was ready to go for the meeting tomorrow?"

We'd managed to land a huge contract on a new skyscraper downtown. Not only does the company stand to make an absurd amount of money if everything goes well, but it would make me look like a fucking genius to the board of directors.

"It's Chandler, from the city. There's been a last-minute zoning change. This throws off the whole presentation." The presentation I spent two weeks building—thinking through every contingency and rebuttal. I could have given that presentation in my sleep, and now I'll need to rework the entire fucking thing.

I run my hands through my hair, deciding how I want to play this. I didn't become CEO by wallowing about things that are out of my control. There's nothing to do besides deal with this setback, and really that's all it is. A setback, and one that I'm sure can be overcome.

Before I do anything else, I buzz Noelle.

"Noelle, can you bring me some tea? It looks like I'm going to be here late tonight."

"Right away, Mr. Bennett," she says, and my cock twitches. *Jesus*. Even the way she says my name gets me going. Somehow her low, sultry voice can make even discussing the weather sound like dirty talk.

I send off a quick response to Chandler's email and then look up to see Jamie smirking at me.

"What is it?" I ask, my irritation clear. I'm already on edge about this presentation; the last thing I need is Jamie giving me more lectures about being less uptight.

"Liam, listen to me," he says, standing and stretching. "You don't need caffeine; you need a blow job." Unfortunately, in the middle of his sentence the door swings open and in walks Noelle, holding a steaming mug.

As usual, the sight of her sends all kinds of sinful thoughts shooting through my veins, and more specifically to my dick. I've never looked twice at my assistants, or any of my employees, never wanting to cross that line. But when Noelle walks into my office wearing a blouse that hugs her ample tits and accentuates her trim waist, I have a hard time looking away. To cope, I decide to look at Jamie, but not before I realize that Noelle has heard Jamie's comment. A deep red flush rises in her cheeks, but she keeps walking, her heels clicking as she approaches me.

"Um, here's the tea you asked for," she says, quickly setting it down on the desk in front of me before turning to leave. I catch a whiff of something soft and floral, like lavender and rose, before she walks away, which distracts me all over again. I watch her shut the door, unable to stop myself from noticing the way her black skirt hugs her round ass, which would be the perfect size for me to grab onto while she rides my…

"Hello?" Jamie says, waving a hand at me. *Fuck.* What's my problem? I need to keep it together around Noelle, at least until this presentation is over with.

"Can you not talk about blow jobs in the office?

This is a business, not a frat house," I snap at him, a little more harshly than I meant to.

Jamie holds his hands up and shakes his head.

"This reaction is exactly why you need to get laid," he responds, unshaken by my sharp tone. By now, he's used to dealing with my type-A personality. "Just think about that date."

For a moment, I wonder if Jamie is right. I've definitely shut myself off to women lately, and even though it might help to get back out into the dating world, it sounds horrible. Watching the person you'd planned to spend the rest of your life with turn into someone you don't recognize kind of takes the wind out of your sails. Plus, getting cheated on doesn't help, and knowing it was because of all the long hours I spend at work makes it even worse. All I've wanted since the divorce is to focus on work and my kids, who are a lot more important than a quickie with some woman Jamie met at the gym.

Once Jamie leaves, I scrub my hands through my hair and sigh. I need to apologize to Noelle for what she overheard. That was totally unprofessional. I press the intercom button and call Noelle back into my office. She's totally composed after the incident, which is one great thing about her. In fact, she's the best fucking assistant I've ever had, always one step ahead of me, as if she knows what I need before I do. The last thing I want to do is scare her off the job because of some stupid comment by Jamie.

She steps into the room and my gut twitches. Her tits bounce slightly as she takes a seat in the chair in front of me, but I keep my eyes locked on hers. If there's one thing I've learned in my years of climbing my way up the corporate ladder, it's the importance of strong eye contact. Which I'll need to distract me from the sexy, irresistible woman sitting five feet away from me. The only trouble is, staring into her deep, honey colored eyes is almost more overwhelming than staring at the rest of her. It's like I can see everything she's thinking before she even opens her mouth to speak.

I clear my throat and look down at my desk for a moment to compose myself, then back up at her.

"I wanted to apologize for anything you overheard a moment ago," I say, all business. I don't think Noelle has any idea exactly how attracted I am to her, which is how I want it, and how it has to be. The last thing I need is for her to feel uncomfortable around me. "Jamie can be a little…" I trail off.

"Adolescent?" she says, then chews on her lower lip. She watches me, gauging my reaction. Little does she know, I appreciate honesty, and a sharp tongue.

"Yes, that," I say, leaning back in my chair, smirking. "But this is a professional workplace, and I don't want you to think that's the kind of thing we encourage here at Griffin."

She nods, brushing her wavy, dark hair back behind one slim shoulder. I catch the scent of her shampoo, something flowery, and all I want to do is grab a fistful of that hair as I push her up against the wall and kiss her. I shake my head, bringing myself back to the moment. There's more we need to discuss, and it's not the easiest subject.

I sigh, then come out with it.

"I also want to discuss the incident from yesterday. The messages I saw on your phone."

I can tell she was hoping we wouldn't have to discuss it again based on the slight redness in her cheeks. Jesus, why does seeing her blush turn me on so much?

"I don't encourage inter-office relationships of any nature." I pause. She hasn't said anything, and it's clear that she's mortified by the conversation. I decide to change my tactic and lighten up a little. "That being said, I'm a human being and I understand that sometimes people are going to be attracted to each other. It doesn't mean we can't still have a successful working relationship, as long as we're both willing to be professional."

She's nodding, her full lips parting into a careful smile. It's impossible not to imagine kissing those lips, or how it would feel to have them wrapped around my cock. My desk is large enough that if she kneeled underneath it, someone walking by would have no idea what was happening. I let out a grunt that I try to conceal as a cough and shift in my chair, the ache in my gut growing stronger by the second.

"I agree," she says, oblivious to the reaction I'm having to her—thank God. "And I'm sorry about the texts. Let's keep it professional. I'm here to help you in any way I can, and that includes staying late tonight if you could use the help."

I nod, glad we've cleared the air. As uncomfortable as a conversation like this can be, I'm not the kind of guy who runs from anything. I just need to remind myself, as much as her, to stay professional. And that means not imagining my assistant giving me a blow job in the middle of a work day.

As I watch Noelle leave the room, I vow to keep all indecent thoughts from my mind. But then, I feel a sinking sensation in the pit of my stomach. Because I realize I'm going to be in the office, at night, alone with Noelle. Not much scares me, but this is new territory. I'm a man who likes to plan, but fate just threw me a curve ball I never saw coming.

CHAPTER THREE

Noelle

I stand up to stretch my legs, having kicked off my heels hours ago. I glance over at Liam, who is totally absorbed in his work—no surprise there—the white glow of the computer screen highlighting his square jawline. He even looks yummy deep in concentration.

I wasn't exactly thrilled at the idea of working late, but it's actually been nice to work alongside Liam after hours. I didn't think he'd ever heard of the term "relax" before, but he's loosened his tie and undone the top buttons of his shirt. We've even had a little casual conversation that didn't have to do with work. Plus, with his shirt unbuttoned, when he shifts in his seat, his shirt strains enticingly across his well-defined pecs. I don't hate it.

Not in the least.

I swallow and force myself to look away. I should really be focusing on the presentation, and not on checking out my hot boss. To distract myself, I check the time.

"Oh, I didn't realize it was already so late." Liam raises his head at my voice, and I point to the clock. It's well past eight o'clock. "Should we order some dinner? I think we might be here for a while."

He nods. "Brilliant idea. And thanks again for staying so late," he says, looking up from his work. I feel a lightning bolt shoot into my stomach when our eyes connect. "I'm sure you have other things you'd rather be doing."

Like you? I think and bite my tongue. We agreed to keep things professional less than six hours ago and I'm already having a hard time keeping my thoughts clean. What's wrong with me?

It would be a lot easier to keep my mind on work if I weren't so painfully aware of the fact that Liam and I are alone, at night, in his office, less than ten feet away from each other. This is basically the beginning of every one of my fantasies about him, and I'm having a hard time stopping myself from making one of them come to life.

"Yeah, I'm pretty upset that you ruined my big plan to watch *You've Got Mail* with a pint of ice cream," I say sarcastically, smirking at him. "But I'm sure you can think of a way to make it up to me."

Shit, did I say that out loud? I need to keep it together, and flirting with him isn't going to make it any easier to ignore my very obvious attraction to him.

I'm afraid he's going to scold me for crossing a line, but instead he smirks back at me.

"I can think of a few ways," he says quietly, and my heart skips a beat. I swallow, and our eyes meet. Just looking into those emerald eyes sends a wave of lust through me, and I have to pull my gaze away before I decide to forget about our conversation earlier and throw myself on top of him.

I clear my throat and focus. "So, what should we order? Chinese?"

"Whatever you want is fine with me," he tells me, looking back at his laptop.

Unfortunately, what I really want right now can't be ordered at a Chinese restaurant.

I head into the hallway to make the phone call, hoping a break from Liam will ease the sexual tension between us.

After I place the order, I try to look at my computer, but I'm going cross-eyed from information overload.

"I need a drink," I mutter, pulling open another file.

Liam looks up, raising an eyebrow.

"Oh, sorry, not that I'm not enjoying the work, I'm just a little beat," I say quickly. *Come on, Noelle, try to have a filter.*

To my surprise, Liam smiles. "I think we could make a drink happen," he says quietly. He stands up and walks to the wall, where there's a small hutch I've never paid attention to before. He pulls it open and a light comes on inside, revealing several bottles of whiskey and four rocks glasses set on a shelf.

I snort. "What are you, James Bond or something?"

He lets out a low laugh, and I realize it's one of the first times I've heard it. Before tonight, I thought Liam might be an actual robot. But as much as it turns me on to have him bossing me around, I'm finding myself more and more interested in this other, more laid-back side of him. I really had no idea this side even existed.

He pours us each a glass of whiskey and walks over to hand me one.

Just having him near me makes me feel like my heart is going to explode. As I take the glass from him my fingers brush his hand. I've never had such a strong physical reaction to someone before, and I take a big gulp of the whiskey to distract myself. I know mixing alcohol with my attraction to Liam is probably a lethal combination, but desperate times call for desperate measures.

We work quietly, the click of the keys and the low hum of fluorescent lights the only sound.

"Shit," Liam says, shuffling through files on his desk. "Where did I put that zoning map?"

"You left it on the side table," I tell him, nodding toward it.

"Why would I have put it on the…" he trails off as he walks over and picks up the map from the table.

"I forgot, thanks," he says quietly, looking up

at me.

"That's what I'm here for," I say brightly, smiling at him. Inappropriate attraction aside, Liam and I do make a great team at work. We've been in sync about almost everything on this presentation, and even though I can tell he's nervous about it, I know he's going to do an amazing job.

By now, the alcohol has started to make me slightly lightheaded. I glance up at Liam, who's still hard at work, and decide we need to loosen things up a little bit.

"Alright, I think we deserve a break," I say, setting my drink down a little harder than I meant to. It probably doesn't help that I'm drinking on an empty stomach. "Let's do something fun, then we'll put the last touches on the presentation."

Liam hesitates, glancing at his computer.

I stand up and slowly walk over to him. He watches me silently, and with every step I feel my heart pounding harder against my chest. The alcohol must be strong, because I have no inhibitions about perching on the edge of his desk and crossing my legs, my thigh just a foot away from his hand. When I sit down, I see his eyes travel from my legs up to my eyes, and I can't control the shiver that runs through my body.

Liam's still watching me, and as much as I want to slide off the desk and straddle him, I force myself to stay where I am. It's totally boring and very adult-like of me.

He still hasn't responded and he's still watching me with that laser-like focus he uses when he's trying to solve a difficult problem.

"Come on, when's the last time you did something fun?" I tease, breaking the silence and grinning at him.

Finally, he smiles, revealing straight, white teeth. "Honestly, I can't even remember," he says, closing his laptop.

I hop off the desk.

"Perfect, how about Truth or Dare? I know it's juvenile, but trust me, it'll be fun."

He's watching me, and I wonder if he thinks I'm nuts. Then he stands up.

"Okay, fine," he says, leveling his stare at me. "I pick dare."

"Dare," I repeat, grinning at him. "Okay." I ponder my options, my brain working overtime for something a little sexy, and a lot daring. "I dare you to streak through the office."

He snorts and shakes his head. "Seriously? Streaking? You know there are cameras out there, right?"

"You're the one who picked dare," I say with a shrug. "If you're too afraid to streak, I could give you a new dare. But if I do that, there's no turning back."

He processes this, and finally shakes his head. Streaking was probably a little too much.

"I can handle it," he says, his eyes boring into mine. I'm suddenly too aware of how close Liam's body is to mine, and my stomach does several backflips. His voice is low and husky when he asks, "What's the new dare?"

My heart is pounding so hard against my chest I can hardly breathe. Every logical part of me knows we should stop this, just go back to work and pretend none of it ever happened. But the alcohol and my desire are stronger than logic.

"Kiss me," I say, looking back into his eyes. Even after I say it, I can't really believe the words just left my mouth. I just dared my boss, the CEO of this company, to kiss me.

Real fucking smooth, Noelle.

His expression is serious, his jaw set. My heart sinks, and I wonder if I've gone too far. But then he nods.

"It's a dare, so I guess I have to do it," he says, a small smile playing across his full lips.

"Those are the rules. And we can't break the rules," I say, slightly breathless, as he takes a step toward me.

He takes another step so that he's standing right in front of me. His masculine scent fills my nostrils, intoxicating me. He lifts a hand to tilt my chin up, so that I'm looking directly into his eyes, and I feel my knees go weak. When his lips press against mine, it's like there's a fire inside of me, and I step in closer so that our bodies are pressed together. He slides a hand onto the small of my back, pulling me against him, and I let out a whimper. He slides his tongue into my mouth, teasing me, and I arch my back slightly so that my breasts are pressed into his chest. I slide my hands up his torso, feeling his toned body underneath his shirt. And just when I think I can't take it, that I need him *all up in my inbox* right now, he pulls away.

"Noelle, we can't," he says, and the way my

name sounds in his mouth is so silky and rich.

I take a moment to catch my breath, and we stare at each other, still close enough to touch, when my phone starts ringing. I jump, startled by the interruption, and run to answer it. It's the food delivery, waiting by the reception desk. I quickly walk to grab the food, hoping I look composed enough that the delivery guy can't tell I was just making out with my boss.

When I walk back into Liam's office and set the food down, I'm still a little shaky, and I can tell he is, too. Usually, he's totally put together, but it's clear our kiss has shaken him up.

"You like the spicy noodles, right?" I ask, desperately trying to talk about something normal. Clearly, I'm not very well versed in the best way to speak to your boss moments after you've stuck your tongue down his throat.

"Right," he says, taking the box from me. We start eating in silence, and after a few minutes I can't take it anymore.

"I guess we should probably finish the presentation," I say, trying to ease the tension. Focusing on work is the only thing I can think of to distract me from the sinking feeling in my stomach. While

I'm a little hurt, and definitely experiencing lady blue balls, I get why Liam put a stop to the kiss. The best way to deal with it now is to get the presentation done so we can both go home and pretend it never happened.

"I think there are just a few more small kinks to work out, and then we can get out of here," he says, pulling out a new file. He glances at it for a moment, then looks back over at me, his eyes moving up and down my body.

"Fuck it," he says, throwing down the file. He walks around the desk and pulls me up against him. He presses his lips to mine, harder this time, and more frenzied. I can taste the whiskey on his tongue.

He lifts me up and sets me down on his desk roughly. I spread my legs open and grab onto his shirt, pulling him in. Then we're kissing again, his hands pulling my blouse out from my skirt and sliding up to trail along my stomach. I can feel my nipples pebble as his fingers inch toward my breasts, and I arch my back as he moves to kiss my neck.

Working alongside him every day for the past three months has been a huge test to my willpower.

I want Liam more than I've ever wanted some-one before, and right about now I'm having a hard time remembering why we should stop.

CHAPTER FOUR

Liam

Noelle is in my arms, making tiny need-filled whimpers as I suck on her tongue. It's been way too long since I've had any action, and I can see now that was a huge mistake on my part. I know I should put a stop to this, but she feels so good rubbing herself against my chest.

While her hands curl, grabbing fistfuls of my shirt to hold me close, I push my fingers into the silky strands of her hair. I slide a hand up her neck and take her hair in my fist, something I've imagined doing every time she wears it down. I gently bite her bottom lip and she moans, the sound sending white hot electricity straight to my groin.

I want her more than I've ever wanted someone before, and I know I should put a stop to what we're doing, but it's like every dirty fantasy I've had for the past three months is finally coming to life.

I pull Noelle tighter against me. The feel of her breasts pushed against my chest almost sends me over the edge. Jamie was right—it's been way too long since I've been with a woman. And if cutting loose feels this good, then I need to do it *way* more often.

Our kisses become more frantic, and I feel a familiar pressure behind my zipper. As we kiss, she undoes the buttons of my shirt, pulling it open and running her hands along my chest. She lets a finger slide south, close to my waistband and I let out a groan.

"You have no idea how long I've wanted to do this," she says, pulling back to look me up and down.

"I think I might have an idea." I lift her up in my arms and she lets out a little gasp that goes straight to my balls. "I should punish you for distracting me so much at work," I say, easing her down onto the small leather couch beneath the windows.

"I could say the same to you," she says with a

sly smile, grabbing the sides of my open shirt in her fists and pulling me on top of her.

I reach for the buttons of her blouse, purposely taking my time. She breathes heavily, watching me with those big eyes. I pull the blouse back to reveal a lacy black bra that leaves little to the imagination. I inhale sharply at the sight of her round breasts, kissing between them and running my tongue along the edge of the lace, teasing her. I can feel her heart beating hard and fast. I move down to kiss along her stomach, and along the edge of her skirt.

"Take it off," she pleads. She wants this as much as I do, and the sight of that skirt hugging her full hips has been teasing me all day. I don't waste any time unzipping it and pulling it down to reveal lace panties that match her bra.

"Do you always wear lingerie like this to work?" I ask. It's none of my business, but part of me needs to know. That little tidbit of information will fuel future fantasies of mine.

She always dresses so professionally, and it drives me wild to think she's been hiding this beneath her tailored suits and fitted trousers the whole time.

"Maybe I was hoping someone would see it,"

she says with a smile, her voice heavy with desire. She pulls me in close again, reaching for the zipper of my pants.

"Patience," I tell her, voice firm.

She watches me in fascination as I gently press her legs open, moving between them and kissing along her inner thigh. Finally, she leans back, and I relish the way her hips rock with eagerness. I run my tongue along the edge of her black lacy knickers, then bite onto them and pull them to the side. I take in the sight of her, and we're both breathing heavily. She's waxed completely bare and I'll never be able to *not* picture this when I'm working beside her. *Fuck*.

God bless American women.

I breathe in the feminine scent of her, my cock hardening impossibly more, then strategically place wet, sucking kisses everywhere except for where she wants me.

Noelle groans in frustration. Her fingers push into my hair, rucking it up, but I couldn't give two fucks. We've been building toward this moment for three long months.

When I finally slide my tongue gently along her warm, silken center, she cries out. The sound of it sends me into a frenzy and I work her over faster, lapping her up until she's trembling.

Her body rocks against me so much that I have to use an arm to hold her hips in place, which only turns her on more, her small moans growing louder and louder. I slide my other hand up and slip it underneath her bra, gently pinching her nipple between my fingers. She lets out a loud cry at my touch and writhes beneath me. Her reaction to me is almost enough to make me come myself, and I can feel my erection pressing into the front of my trousers almost painfully.

I move my tongue faster as her moans grow louder, and then she arches her back and cries out, the wave of her orgasm flowing through her and against my mouth. I slow the movement of my tongue to match the tensing of her body, and once she relaxes beneath me I rest my head on her thigh.

"You're good at that," she says in wonder, still almost gasping for air.

Before I can reply, I hear the squeaky wheel of a cart in the hallway. We both sit up, and realize the cleaning crew has come in. I quickly help her find her clothes before buttoning my shirt, and just as she's zipped up her skirt the cleaning woman steps into the room.

"Oh, sorry, I didn't mean to interrupt," she says, looking between us. The small smile on her lips lets me know she's completely aware of what just happened between Noelle and I. I clear my throat loudly.

"You're not interrupting, just give us a minute to pack up our things and we'll be out of your way," I say gruffly. Not much throws me off, but almost getting caught feasting on my assistant might be the exception.

Bloody hell.

The cleaning woman nods, still smirking, and moves to clean the next office.

Noelle and I look at each other when she leaves, and then we burst out laughing. I can't believe how good it feels to laugh with her. Never mind sex, I realize it's been years since I've been around a woman I can relax and have fun with.

With my ex, there was always arguing and accusations, but I'm realizing that not all relationships have to be that way. I look at Noelle as she packs files back into the cabinets, watching her move about my office while my brain spins. I've never met someone so carefree and full of life, and I never expected it to happen at work.

She turns, catching me staring at her. "What?" she asks, smiling slightly.

I shake my head, walking behind my desk.

"Nothing," I tell her, picking up my bag. "It's late. We should call it a night."

She nods, and we grab our things and head to the elevators. It's late and we're the last ones to leave the building. Once the elevator doors shut, I step closer to Noelle, breathing her in. Her usual scent is mixed with the heavier scent of sex, and I feel a familiar pressure between my legs at the memory of tasting her.

I take in the slight flush of her cheeks and her lips, which look even fuller than usual from our frantic kissing. She notices me staring and smiles up at me with those honey eyes. I slide an arm around her hips and pull her in close. When our lips touch a jolt runs through my body, and I have to stop myself from taking things farther.

"Are you okay?" I ask.

She nods, meeting my eyes. "I'm very okay. As long as you're not going to fire me tomorrow?"

My brows pinch together. That's what she thinks of me? I'd be a complete arsehole to terminate her over what just happened. We both got swept away in the moment, and even though I should, I can't seem to make myself regret it.

"You're most definitely not fired. In fact, you may be due for a raise."

She ducks her head, blushing slightly as the elevator slows to a stop, the doors opening with a ping, before saying, "I'd say you are due for a *raise* yourself."

"Touché, Ms. St. James."

We exit together and head toward the massive glass doors.

"I'll see you tomorrow," she says, looking up at me from under her long eyelashes.

I nod, wishing I was taking her home with me. As I walk to my car, the memory of touching her clouds all other judgment. Not only is Noelle sexier than I'd ever imagined, she's also smart and fun to be with. What just happened between us may have been wrong, but I've never felt more right about anything in my entire life.

The next morning, I force thoughts of Noelle from my head as I deliver the presentation. The last thing I need is to sprout a boner in the middle of the most important presentation of my life. Luckily for me, it goes better than I could have imagined. With Noelle's help, I was able to put together a proposal that's going to net the company millions of dollars.

With that out of the way, there's just one more thing I need to take care of.

As I leave the meeting, I pass Noelle at her desk.

"Noelle, a word?" I ask tersely. Despite what happened last night, I'm trying to keep it professional during the workday. Even though all I want to do is pull off her dress and finish what we started.

She follows me into my office, closing the door behind her. She's wearing a black dress that hugs her curves and a pair of high, black heels that accentuate her long, toned legs. I've never thought much about the term fuck me heels before, but I think I'm starting to catch on. I shake my head, trying to keep my mind on the task at hand. I don't know what Noelle is feeling after last night, and I don't want to make any assumptions if she has regrets.

Once we're tucked inside my office, I close the door and turn to face her.

"I just wanted to check in with you after what happened last night," I say quietly, standing close to her. Her hair is down today, her dark waves bouncing each time she moves her head. The sight of it sends a pang of desire straight to my cock, which I do my best to ignore. "Are you okay?"

"Are you asking if I'm freaked out that my boss went down on me in his office after hours and that we were almost caught by the cleaning crew?" she asks. "That's just a typical Wednesday night for me," she says sarcastically, grinning. She's wearing red lipstick today that makes her full lips look even more irresistible.

I laugh, tucking a strand of hair behind her ear.

"I like you," I tell her, losing myself for a moment in her honey eyes. "You're honest, and funny, and to be frank, I haven't had much fun in a long time."

She seems taken aback by my bluntness for a moment, but quickly recovers. "Forgive me for asking," she says, looking up at me. "But are the rumors about your divorce true?"

I nod, running a hand along her bare arm. I feel

goose bumps erupt at my touch.

"My marriage was over a long time ago. But we officially filed the papers a few months before you started working here." I pause, knowing I have to continue but wishing this situation could be less complicated.

"I have three kids. My life is messy. But I like you, and for once in my life I want to do something because I want to, and not just because I'm supposed to."

I watch her closely, trying to gauge her reaction. I know it's a risk to lay it all out like this, but I need to be with a woman who can handle my baggage.

She bites her lip. "Won't that complicate things at work?"

I let out a small laugh. "Probably, but what's life without a little complication?"

"Well, I never thought I'd see the day you'd be convincing *me* to have more fun," she says with a smirk. "Okay, I'm in. What did you have in mind?"

"How about a date? This Saturday night. And I mean a real date, not just Chinese food in my office," I say, voice softening.

Her full lips part into a full smile. "I think I could do that."

"So, it's a date, then," I say, and she looks around before giving my hand a quick squeeze. I watch her leave my office, her hips swaying seductively in her tight dress. Jesus, even the way she walks makes me want to fuck her.

Long after Noelle has left my office and I've returned to work, I realize I'm still smiling. I might be about to make a huge mistake, but for the first time in my life I don't feel the need to micromanage the situation. So far, things with Noelle have been better than I could have imagined. As unexpected as it is, I can't deny my attraction to this woman.

CHAPTER FIVE

Noelle

"You fucked your boss?" Maxine practically screams across the crowded bar. A few heads turn in our direction, and I cover my face with my hands.

It's Friday night at our favorite bar downtown, and now, thanks to Maxine, I can never come here again.

"Can you keep it down?" I hiss between my fingers. "I don't need everyone within a five-mile radius to know about this. Besides, we didn't have sex."

"Yeah, even better, you got off and didn't have to do anything in return." Maxine raises a hand to high five me, and I ignore her.

"So, was it good?" Jess asks at a more appropriate volume, sipping her vodka soda.

"Beyond good," I say, unable to keep the grin off my face. And it was. The memory of his tongue running down my body keeps popping into my head at random times, making me shiver and sending chills straight between my legs. In fact, I don't think I've ever had an orgasm that intense before. Usually the first time is a little awkward, but with Liam things flowed so naturally. Even talking about it now with my friends makes me feel a little hot and bothered. And tomorrow we'll be going on a date, and, with any luck, finally having the mindblowing sex I've been imagining for months.

Oh my God, am I crazy?

"Well I'm jealous," Maxine pouts, bringing me back to reality. "I haven't had sex in forever."

"I thought you hooked up with that guy from Tinder last weekend?" I point out, raising an eyebrow.

Maxine pauses thoughtfully for a moment, then shrugs. "Yeah but that was a week ago." She cranes her neck around the bar. "Now I'm looking for someone new. There has to be at least one cute guy here."

"Was it awkward at work the next day?" Jess asks as Maxine smiles flirtatiously at a man across the bar.

"Honestly, no. Things have been great," I tell her. After Liam checked in with me to make sure I was okay, any anxiety I had about what happened between us melted away. He isn't some creep who's just trying to get laid; he's sweet and thoughtful. Plus, every time I walk into his office the memories of that night come flooding back. It feels like we've been having secret extended foreplay session all week. I've never felt this kind of anticipation before, and by this morning I was so horny I was ready to pull my clothes off and jump on top of him in front of everyone. Thankfully, I managed not to. Yay, me.

"You haven't told us the most important thing," Maxine says, giving up on trying to flirt. "How big was his, you know?" She grins slyly.

"I'm not telling you that," I say, playfully slapping her away. "Besides, I didn't even see it yet."

"You haven't seen his dick?" Maxine says loudly again. A few people nearby turn to stare.

"Can you control yourself?" I ask her, unable to stop myself from laughing even through my mortification. "I'd like to be able to show my face here again. Besides, I'll probably see it tomorrow."

"Tomorrow?" they practically gasp in unison.

"You're going to see him outside of work?" Jess asks, lowering her voice like she's discussing top secret information.

I grin, sipping my martini.

"Yeah, why not? It's not like it's illegal to spend your free time with your boss. Especially since he's the one who asked me out."

"It just seems so…" Jess trails off.

"Naughty," Maxine says, smirking at me. "I'm so proud of you."

"You'll be even more proud of me after tomorrow night," I tell her with a wink.

Maxine laughs and Jess shakes her head, grinning. I can't believe this is actually happening. I'm finally going to sleep with my boss, consequences be damned.

I run my fingers through my hair, tousling it to accentuate my dark waves. It's a few hours before our date, and I've been a wild mixture of nervous and excited all day. All of my easy confidence from last night is gone, and I keep thinking about everything that could go wrong. Sure, Liam and I make a great team at work, but what about in the real world? I've never even seen him outside the confines of the office, just the two of us. *Alone*.

Plus, I'm still so turned on by the thought of him that I'm not sure I'll be able to focus on conversation. Especially since that conversation will be spoken in his hot-as-sin accent.

I'd gone to hot yoga earlier to calm my nerves but every pose, from downward dog to pigeon, just made me think about all of the positions I want to try with Liam.

I slide a bit of rosy matte lipstick across my lips and apply a touch of mascara. As I pucker my lips the memory of Liam kissing me in his office flashes through my mind, and heat shoots through me. I breathe deeply, trying to refocus. I need to concentrate on getting through the date and stop getting so ahead of myself. Unfortunately, it's easier said than done. It's just a little difficult to focus when you're about to sleep with the sexiest man you've ever seen, who also happens to be your boss.

I head into my room to pick out an outfit, settling on a silky blue dress that accentuates my curves. It's the perfect combination of sexy and classy. I don't want it to be too obvious, but I also don't mind sending Liam a subtle hint that I'm ready to take things to the next level. I slip on my lucky lingerie set before the dress, checking myself in the mirror. Liam will be here soon, and my heart is moving a mile a minute.

Despite my nervousness, deep down I feel like things are going to go well. Being around Liam is definitely a hormonal roller-coaster, but there's something about him that makes me feel like everything about our taboo hookup is going to be okay. Our relationship might not be conventional, but he's definitely the most put-together guy I've seen in a while.

I guess there's no turning back after this. Liam and I are about to find out once and for all if this thing between us could be more than just an office fling.

CHAPTER SIX

Liam

"**D**ad, can we stay longer?" Charlie asks, licking the last drops of syrup off his fingers.

"Sorry, buddy, but we have to get you back to your mom's house," I tell him, reaching over to wipe his face with a napkin.

It's Lexi's weekend with the kids, and if I drop them off late again, she's going to fly off the handle.

"Mom won't be mad," he whines, curling up in his chair.

I almost want to laugh, since that's the understatement of the year, but I plaster a smile on and ruffle his hair.

"We'll hang out next week, okay?"

Charlie nods sadly. Every time I drop them off at my ex's house, it breaks my heart. I'd never say anything bad about her in front of them, but as human beings go, she's one of the more vindictive ones I've met.

Of course, she waited until after I'd put a ring on it to show me that side of her.

I finish cleaning up the mess from the homemade waffles I made the kids for breakfast, then I kneel down on the floor to inspect the twins, cleaning off their faces and adjusting their dresses. If even one hair is out of place, I'm going to get an earful from Lexi about my negligent parenting.

"Okay everybody, let's get off then," I say, lifting the twins and slinging their overnight bag over one shoulder.

As we drive to their mom's house I put on the latest *Disney* soundtrack they're obsessed with. Charlie can't get enough of it, pretending to play a guitar as he sings along.

"Dad, sing with me," he begs, and finally I give in, belting out the theme song like I'm Bruno Mars. Charlie has a way of getting me to loosen up, and after a long tense week at the office there's nothing better than spending time with him and the girls. I don't want the ride to end, but soon enough we pull up to the house.

Lexi's already waiting by the front door, her arms crossed. I brace myself, sure she's got something on her mind. I'm not easily shaken up, but Lexi has a special talent for making me want to lose my shit. *Good times.*

I help Charlie out of his booster seat and set him on the sidewalk next to the bags before I get the girls out of their car-seats. They each take one of my hands as we head up the sidewalk to the front door.

"You're late," Lexi says, raising an eyebrow.

What did she want me to do? Take their plates away at breakfast before they were finished eating? Bloody hell.

"There was a little traffic. I'm only five minutes late," I say, keeping my tone measured.

She's wearing a fitted green turtleneck that matches her emerald eyes and tight black jeans. Her red hair is pulled up into a ponytail, accentuating her high cheekbones. She looks stunning, but I lost the ability to see her beauty a long time ago. She might look amazing on the outside, but she's got a black hole where her heart is supposed to be.

"Don't let it happen again, okay?" she says sharply.

"Nice to see you, too," I murmur, not wanting

the kids to hear us fighting. Throughout the divorce we did our best to keep the arguments behind closed doors, but Lexi could never resist the opportunity to throw a jab.

"Hi Mom," Charlie says with a grin, running up to give her a hug. I'm glad to see that, despite the less than ideal home situation, he's growing up to be a sweet kid.

I let go of the girls' hands so they can go inside, but they turn and each grab a leg, hanging onto me.

"Stay with us," Olivia says, looking up at me with her big green eyes.

"Please?" Alexis begs.

I'm not a sap, by any means. But seeing my kids beg me to stay with them is almost enough to bring a tear to my eye. I pull them gently from my legs and kneel down to their height.

"Next week I'll take you to the park. And we'll get ice cream," I tell them, kissing each of them on the forehead.

I hug Charlie goodbye and turn to leave after the kids are inside.

"Liam, hang on," Lexi says, lingering at the door. I turn back, wondering if I forgot something.

Lexi sighs. "Please don't make promises you can't keep."

"Excuse me?"

"The park and ice cream?" She raises an eyebrow. "You can't have changed that much. We both know you don't have time for that, not if it might get in the way of work."

She says the last part sarcastically, and I have to take deep breaths to keep my cool. The kids are still lingering near the doorway, and I can only hope they didn't overhear what Lexi said.

It's true that when we were married, I worked a lot and most of the kid-friendly outings were left to her. But that's only because I thought we were a team. I'd been operating under the impression that I was the one working sixty-hour weeks and earning a paycheck so that she could stay at home and our children could attend private schools. I thought we'd both been making those sacrifices for our family. I guess I thought wrong.

I take a deep breath and try to calm myself.

"I'll be back to pick them up next week," I say through my teeth. It takes all of my willpower to turn and walk away without spewing out all of the pent-up frustration I have toward her, but if I've learned anything through my divorce it's that I can't let her comments get to me. In the end, it's the kids who end up hurt by our fighting.

Back in the car, I clench my fists around the steering wheel and take a few deep breaths before driving off. At least I have the date with Noelle to look forward to tonight, or I'd be stewing about this all day.

Just the thought of Noelle makes me feel strangely calm. I haven't been able to get her off my mind all week, and seeing her in the office after what happened between us brightened an otherwise insane work week. Catching eye contact or brushing a hand across hers as we passed each other was enough to keep me in a constant state of desire all week. Not to mention, just the memory of what happened between us still gets me hard.

Jamie's right—I absolutely need to get laid. As much as I enjoyed making Noelle come the other night, I can't stop thinking about what would have happened if we hadn't been interrupted by the cleaning crew. It feels like the last few days have been leading toward tonight, and I'm ready to finish what we started. And if the preview was any indication, the main event is going to be pretty fucking spectacular.

I decide I need some endorphins after my encounter with Lexi and so I head to the gym. I spend an hour blowing off steam, then shower and begin to get ready for our date. I'm normally not a huge romantic, but I booked us reservations at the nicest steakhouse in town and made special arrangements to have a wine pairing with our meal. I wouldn't usually go this far out on a limb for a first date, but considering the circumstances, I want Noelle to know that she's not just some hookup. We make a really good team, and I hope this date proves that to her.

I pull up to Noelle's apartment at exactly seven. When she comes out the front door, it's like all the air gets sucked out of my Lexus. Damn, she's stunning.

As I step out, I watch her approach, her hips swaying enticingly as she moves closer. I just stand there like a dumbass, appreciating the view.

"Hi there." She stops in front me, grinning.

"Fuck." I straighten. "I mean hello."

Noelle laughs and the sound is light, easy,

beautiful. Just like her.

As crazy as it sounds, she's been my salvation for the past few months. There were so many changes in my life over the past year—separating from my wife of ten years, moving out and into a new home, working even more hours just to fill the empty void inside me—and then my assistant left and I hired Noelle. And little by little, everything started to change.

She's been a breath of fresh air for me. I can see that now—it's clearer than ever that I'm no longer clouded, trying to hide my attraction for her.

"You look beautiful," I tell her, and I mean it. She always looks stunning, but there's something about her tonight that's even more alluring. She's wearing a fitted blue dress and a pair of nude heels, and her hair cascades onto her tan shoulders in dark waves.

"That's quite a dress," I add. Her full lips part into a smile, and I can't stop myself from imagining how it's going to feel to have those lips kissing my chest, down my stomach and all the way to my cock. I clear my throat. *Get a grip*, I warn myself. *The date just started.*

"This old thing?" she says sarcastically. "I just

found it in the bottom of my closet."

I laugh, relieved that there's no first-date tension.

I offer her my arm and walk her over to the car door, opening it for her. The neckline of her dress is just low enough that I can see her full tits bouncing with each step. I feel a pressure in my groin as she leans in to hug me, her breasts pressing against my chest. My cock twitches as she turns to get in the car and I catch a glimpse of her ass.

Inside the car, she crosses one long, toned leg over the other, and tosses her hair back. The scent of her fresh, clean shampoo hits me and I inhale. *God, how does she always smell so good?* I want to grab onto her hair and pull her against me, but I stop myself. *Get a grip, Liam.* I'm a thirty-five-year-old man; I need to stop acting like a teenage boy about to lose his virginity. This night isn't just about sex, it's about getting to know each other. And we're not going to be able to do that if all I can do is think about what's underneath her dress.

We pull up to the restaurant and I hand the keys to the valet. As we're walking to our table I notice multiple guys turning to stare at Noelle. Far from the jealous type, I don't mind the stares. In fact, I completely understand. Noelle's the kind of woman who lights up every room she enters. She could walk into the restaurant wearing sweatpants and a t-shirt and she'd still be turning heads.

"I've always wanted to come here," she says excitedly after we've placed our drink orders. "Thanks for asking me to come out. It's nice to spend some time together when we don't have to do work."

I nod. "Don't thank me. You're the one who made me realize I need to relax once in a while."

She smiles at me across the table and I feel an ache in my gut. The candlelight highlights her high cheekbones and wide, honey colored eyes.

"Let's make a pact. No talking about Griffin Real Estate Investments tonight," she says, looking up at me from under her long lashes.

I raise my glass. "Deal. Cheers to having fun," I say and we clink glasses.

"I've been wondering. What did you want to be when you grew up, initially?" she asks, folding her hands in front of her and leaning forward.

I think for a moment. "I guess I always wanted to be a businessman. I used to read *The Economist* and the *Wall Street Journal* growing up, and it always seemed like the path for me."

She raises an eyebrow. "Seriously? No five-year-old wants to be a businessman. There must have been something else you wanted to do, something silly, when you were really young."

I pause as our server sets down our appetizer, a dozen fresh oysters.

"Well, there was one other thing," I say, grinning sheepishly. "I used to write love poems."

She snorts. "Love poems? Like roses are red, violets are blue?"

I laugh. "It started out that way, but I developed as a writer and moved on to haikus. I even won an amateur poetry contest in third grade."

She grins, her eyes wide.

"That's amazing. Why did you stop?" She pauses, narrowing her eyes playfully. "Or are you secretly a famous poet who's just pretending to be a big shot CEO?"

"Sorry to disappoint, but no," I say, shrugging. "I guess once I got to middle school I got caught up in trying to do well in school, and noticing girls for the first time, I stopped writing them."

"Will you write me a poem?" she asks, taking a sip of her wine.

I shake my head. "Trust me, you don't want a love poem from me. I'm no Hemingway."

"Maybe someday," she says slyly.

"Maybe," I say, looking into her honey eyes. "If you're lucky."

She swats me on the arm playfully.

"And what about you?" I ask, sitting back in my chair. "What did Noelle St. James want to be when she grew up?"

She grins, and a blush rises in her cheeks. "You can't make fun of me," she says.

"I wouldn't dare," I say, holding up my hands.

"Well," she says, pausing for a moment. "I wanted to be a clown."

I snort into my glass of wine.

"Really? Like in a circus?"

She nods. "I used to do clown makeup on myself all the time. I even wore it to a couple of birthday parties in elementary school. Everyone loved it. I was a great clown."

I laugh, imagining a small Noelle blowing up a balloon animal with a red nose on.

"So, what went wrong? Why didn't you go through with it?"

"The older I got, the more the glamour of clown life stopped appealing to me." She grins.

"Well, my son Charlie's birthday is coming up, maybe we can book you," I say. "Get you back in the game."

"Trust me, you couldn't afford me." She winks and I let out another chuckle.

"Speaking of Charlie, tell me about your kids," she says, swallowing an oyster. "Charlie is the oldest, right?"

I nod. "Charlie is five, about to be six. He's a sweetheart. He loves helping his mom around the house and likes to pretend he's taking care of the girls."

Noelle grins, and her eyes light up. The wine is starting to settle in, and I'm feeling lighter than I've felt in a long time.

"And how old are the girls?"

"Olivia and Alexis turned three a few months

ago," I say, taking another sip of my wine. "It's bloody insane how fast they're growing. Those two are going to be a handful. They already have an attitude."

Noelle laughs, a light, playful sound. "My kind of girls," she says. "I hope I get to meet them one day."

"I hope so, too," I say, staring into her warm eyes, alight with genuine interest.

I never imagined her saying she'd want to meet my kids. I'm not sure what to think. Then again, she's probably just being polite—trying to make conversation.

We hold eye contact for a moment, and my heart pounds against my chest. I haven't felt this kind of connection with a woman in a long time. Spending time with Noelle is like taking in a big breath of air after you've been drowning.

The server turns up with the main course, interrupting the moment, and I tear my eyes away from her to thank him. He sets a T-bone steak in front of me and a lobster tail in front of Noelle.

"Mmm," she says as she swallows her first bite. "This is amazing."

Her voice is low and sensual, and I have an immediate flashback to the sound of her moaning in my office while I kissed up her thighs. The hairs on my arms stand on end, and I feel an electric pulse shoot through me. I cough gently, trying to ignore the stirring between my legs.

We chat casually as we finish our meal, and I can't help but notice it's the most I've laughed with someone in years. Usually only my kids can get me to loosen up this much, but Noelle has a special talent for making me feel relaxed and carefree. Which, as the hyper driven CEO of a huge company, is rare.

As the valet pulls the car around, I help Noelle into her seat, our hands brushing momentarily before I shut the door. My heart skips a beat, and I swallow as I head to the driver's side. I've been trying to keep my desire for Noelle in check all night, but it's getting harder and harder. Literally. I'm not sure if she wants to come back to my place, and the last thing I want to do is pressure her. As much as I want her, this has to be something we both feel good about. But Jesus, I'm silently praying she wants to come home with me.

"So," I say as I start the car. "Are you tired? I can drop you back off at your apartment, or …."

She turns to me, leaning forward slightly so that the tops of her breasts peek out over the scooped neckline of her dress.

"I'm not tired," she says breathily.

I meet her eyes, and then lean in close. Planting one hand against the back of her delicate neck, I pull her in close. The moment Noelle's lips touch mine, I'm done for.

She leans forward, grabbing my shirt in a fist, and pulls me toward her. Her tongue tastes sweet from the wine as she slowly slides it into my mouth, teasing me.

Fuck.

I love how direct she is. I want nothing more than to take her home and do all of the things I've been imagining for the past few months.

There are no games, no uncertainty. Our attraction is so combustible, it's as if everything is right there on the surface, ready to explode. I suck her luscious bottom lip, gently nibbling it with my teeth and Noelle makes a hungry noise in the back of her throat.

"You liked that?" I murmur.

She groans again, leaning in for another kiss.

When her hand drifts down the front of my shirt, my ab muscles contract, and when she groans again, the sound goes straight to my dick which is already hard.

I can smell the slightly floral scent of her perfume as her hands explore the muscles in my chest, my stomach. All I want is for her to unzip my trousers and wrap those beautiful lips around my cock.

I know I should get us out of here, drive us someplace more private, but I'm not done kissing her. Who knew kissing could be so much fun? A guy deprived of intimacy for the last year, that's who. I'm more than happy to make up for lost time with this beautiful, eager girl.

"You make me crazy," I murmur, finally breaking our kiss, only to move on to sucking on the soft skin of her neck.

"Liam," she rasps.

"Come home with me." It's not a question, but Noelle nods, touching the pad of her finger to her lips as she pulls away, her wide eyes on mine.

We're quiet on the drive home, the sexual tension heavy in the air. I imagine Noelle is thinking exactly what I'm thinking, at least I hope she is and that she's not having any regrets.

When we pull into my driveway Noelle gasps.

"*This* is where you live?" she asks, her jaw dropping.

"It's a little excessive, considering I'm alone here half the time," I say sheepishly. I've gotten used to my huge, six-bedroom house, but it's an imposing sight, resting on the top of a hill at the end of a winding driveway.

"I love all the windows," she says as we step out of the car and approach the front door.

I nod. "That's one thing I told the architect I wanted. Lots of natural light."

I pull open the door and we step inside. Noelle marvels at the two-story entryway, looking up at the chandelier. I walk up behind her and wrap an arm around her waist, pulling her ass into my groin. I'm still aroused, and Noelle makes an eager sound as she spins to face me.

She lands against me, her hands on my chest. I take a step forward until she's pressed against the wall, her body hugging against mine. I tuck a strand of wavy hair behind her ear, running my fingers along her jaw.

"You look so sexy tonight," I mutter, leaning in

to press my lips against hers in a soft kiss. I slide my hand down her curves, cupping her breasts before moving them to her hips. She responds by thrusting her hips against me, and I feel pressure building behind my zipper. She slides her hands up my chest, unbuttoning my shirt and pulling it open. Her hands explore my body, moving down to my stomach, trailing her fingers along the top of my trousers.

"You don't look so bad, either." She smiles shyly.

I nuzzle against her neck, leaving wet, sucking kisses all over her fragrant skin. Noelle's hand wanders lower, finally cupping and rubbing my aching erection right over my pants, and I let out a groan. I grab onto her hand, fighting for some control.

"Naughty girl." I meet her eyes.

"Show me your bedroom?"

"Fuck yes, sweetheart. If that's what you want."

She licks her lips. "I want."

I have to adjust the swollen appendage beside my thigh before I can properly climb the stairs.

Noelle doesn't miss a thing, and lets out a short

laugh. I toss her an amused look over one shoulder that says *your fault*.

Inside my bedroom, I help her onto the large bed, kicking off my shoes before turning to her. She's resting on her elbows, watching me. I can hear her breath coming heavily as I begin kissing her ankles, moving up her legs. I slide her dress up to kiss between her thighs, inhaling sharply at the sight of her lacy red panties. She lays her head back as I kiss right over the center of her panties, continuing to slide her dress up until I pull it over her head. She's wearing a matching bra, her breasts heaving beneath it.

Slowly, I undo the straps of her shoes, keeping eye contact with her as I slide them off. I pull my shirt off and toss it to the side, then lean back over her.

"Tell me what you want," I whisper, pressing a soft, teasing kiss on her full lips.

"You," she says through a moan, tilting her head back to expose her throat. I kiss down her throat and along her shoulders.

"You want my cock, Noelle?" My voice is a harsh pant, but it's the best I can do.

"Mmm," she groans when I lift the fabric of

her bra and slide my tongue over her nipple, which grows hard against my tongue.

"That a yes?"

"Y-yes…."

I groan against her, reaching a hand underneath her to unclasp her bra, her breasts bouncing free of it as I toss it beside the bed. I cup her breasts, slowly circling my fingers around her nipples, teasing her. Finally, my thumbs graze her nipples, and the sight of her writhing at my touch almost sends me over the edge. She whimpers quietly as I move my mouth to her breasts, gently tugging her nipple between my teeth. I move to the other side, giving each breast the attention it deserves.

I start to kiss down her stomach but she sits up abruptly and reaches for my belt, sliding it off in one quick motion. The ache in my groin is almost too much, and I stand up to pull off my pants, and then my boxer briefs. Far from being shy, she openly takes in the sight of my erection as I climb back on top of her and press myself against her. She reaches a hand down to stroke my length, and I let out a groan of pleasure as she runs a finger over the tip.

"Take these off," I order gruffly, tugging at her

panties.

"Thought you'd never ask," she says in a low voice, pulling them off and throwing them to the side. I hover over her for a moment, allowing the anticipation to build. I feel like I might explode, and I savor the feeling for a moment. Then, I rub the tip of my erection against her wetness, my heart pounding harder as I feel how much she wants me.

"So perfect. So wet," I say quietly, trying to control myself.

She arches her back as I continue to press myself against her gently.

"I want you inside me," she whispers.

I roll away from her briefly to grab a condom, and once it's been sufficiently wrestled onto my swollen shaft, I'm back, admiring the view of her on my pillows as I move between her thighs.

Noelle lets her knees drop open, and I take one in my hand. My other, aligning myself to her warm, wet center.

Planting the soles of her feet against the mattress, Noelle lifts her hips, shimmying and moving her gorgeous pussy up and down over my erection. It bobs with pleasure.

Wrapping my hands around her slender calves, I push her legs closer to her ribs, as I press forward. The weight of my erection is right there—and I nudge inside, her warmness inviting me in.

My heartbeat pulses wildly as I draw back and then press forward again.

"Liam," she moans, her eyes sinking closed.

"You're so tight," I grunt as I thrust farther inside of her, moving with the rocking of her hips. She moans loudly, taking me in to the hilt. I grab one of her legs and pull it up over my shoulder, burying myself deeper as her breath turns to short gasps. She moves a hand to my shoulder, digging her nails into me.

When I bring my hand to where we're joined, and begin to rub her beautiful pink flesh, Noelle cries out.

"Oh fuck. Liam. Fuck," she moans.

"Yes, sweetheart?"

Her eyes meet mine, and they're half-lidded and filled with lust. "It's so good. You feel so good."

As do you, princess. "You going to come for me? Tell me what you like."

"You," she moans again. "I like *you*. Don't stop."

I wouldn't dream of it. Unable to control the sudden snapping of my hips, I pump into her faster, my thumb still working against her.

I'm getting dangerously close, and am just about to apologize, to admit it's been a while, when Noelle's entire body begins shaking in light tremors.

And then I feel it.

The best feeling in the entire fucking world.

Her tight heat grips me, her entire body clenching as she comes undone. She lets out a cry of pleasure, her body still trembling as I finally begin to let go.

Left with no choice, I fully surrender, riding out the most intense orgasm as her body continues twitching around mine with overstimulation.

I lean down and press a kiss to her parted lips and then carefully withdraw myself from her heat.

Moving from the bed, I dispose of the condom in the bathroom and then rejoin her on the bed, tugging her naked body close. She curls against me, her long hair falling across my chest.

We're both still, quiet other than the sound of our heavy breathing.

"You're incredible, and I'd say that was worth the wait," I say after a minute, turning to gaze down at her.

"Yeah, you definitely lived up to all of my fantasies," she says with a grin.

"Oh, so you've been fantasizing about me?" I ask with a smirk.

"Just a little." She holds up her thumb and forefinger, wrinkling her nose as she laughs.

I bend over to kiss her forehead and lie back against the pillows. It feels so natural to have Noelle here, lying next to me. For once, I didn't overthink something and it turned out better than I could have imagined. I'm not sure how Noelle feels, but I could definitely get used to having her around.

CHAPTER SEVEN

Noelle

"**C**an I get you anything? Water?"

"Water would be great," I tell Liam, rolling over in bed. I watch as he stands, admiring the muscles that ripple down his back as he stretches. Who knew Liam Bennett, CEO and my boss, had such a great butt? I mean, I always figured he did, the way he filled out those thousand dollar suits, but now that I've seen it in the flesh, it definitely lives up to my expectation.

I lie back after he pulls on a pair of shorts, relishing the slight soreness between my legs. The room smells heavily of sex, and I bury my face in one of Liam's pillows, breathing in the musky pine scent of him. He returns with two glasses of water, and I bite my lip as I watch his abs flex as he leans forward to hand one to me. Even after having sex with him, I'm still blown away by his good looks. His hair is tousled, which makes him look even hotter, something I'd thought was impossible. I'm definitely interested in spending more time with this laid back, loosened up Liam.

I sit up, taking the glass of water from him. I'm still naked, but I don't bother covering up. I've always been comfortable with myself, and either he likes what he sees or he doesn't. Either way, I'm not changing.

I set my water down after finishing most of it and realize Liam is staring at me.

"What?" I ask, leaning back on my elbows.

"Don't move," he commands, and the tone of his voice sends my heart into a frenzy. I loved the way he bossed me around in bed earlier and I'm immediately turned on again, the soreness between my legs turning into an aching.

"You're perfect." He climbs onto the end of the bed, pulling my ankles apart. "Spread your legs," he tells me in a husky voice, and I obey, heat running through me.

He begins kissing my ankles, and up my legs until he reaches my thighs. His mouth explores my inner thighs and along my lower belly, and I feel my lady parts responding.

I lie back, letting the feeling of desire wash over me. *We just had sex, why am I already so turned on again?*

He gently kisses me at my center, his tongue just grazing my clit, and I bite my lip as the intensity flows through me. He continues to kiss me gently, teasing me, until I can't stand it anymore.

"Liam," I whimper, moving a hand down to grip his hair in my fist.

He takes the cue, finally running his tongue along the length of my wetness, and I let out a low moan. He moves his tongue faster, focusing on just the right spot. He knows exactly what he's doing, and it doesn't take long before I feel electricity building inside me. I close my eyes, focusing on the feeling of his tongue against me. He pushes my legs wider with his hands so I'm fully open to him, and the pressure inside of me grows. I can hardly breathe, and I let out a loud cry of pleasure as the first wave of my orgasm floods through me, my hips rocking against his mouth. He continues lapping me up until I'm still, my heart pounding against my chest. I'm breathing heavily, my body trembling slightly. But then Liam stands, removing his shorts before climbing back over me.

"How are you already hard again?" I gasp, drinking in the sight of his full nine inches. It's only been twenty minutes since we last had sex.

"It must be you," he says quietly. He stares into my eyes for a moment, and my heart pounds against my chest. "Can I fuck you again?" he asks, pressing his erection against my thigh.

I nod, still hardly able to move from the intensity of my orgasm. Liam bends down to kiss me gently at first, then more hungrily as I slide my tongue into his mouth. He turns me over roughly so I'm on my stomach and begins kissing along my shoulders, then between my shoulder blades and down my spine. A shiver of anticipation runs through me as he grabs my ass in his hands, gripping it before giving it a hard smack. I breathe in sharply, turning to look at him. His eyes are heavy with desire, and I swallow, trying to keep my breath even. He pulls my hips up so I'm on my knees, then presses his erection between my thighs, rubbing his shaft along my wetness.

Dear God … this man. I guess the boardroom isn't the only place he likes to take control.

He reaches his hands around me, cupping my

breasts in his hands before pinching my nipples gently. I gasp, arching my back and pressing myself into him. He continues massaging my breasts, running a finger across my nipple every so often as heat builds inside of me. I whimper again as he presses himself tighter against me, the ache between my legs becoming almost unbearable.

"I want you," I moan, unable to wait any longer.

Liam pulls back, and I hear the crinkle of a wrapper, and then he's pressing the tip of his erection inside of me with a groan. I rock back against him, taking him further in, wanting to feel him fully inside of me. He grabs onto my hips, entering me deeper with each thrust.

He reaches a hand around to my clit, gently rubbing it. I'm almost overcome by the sensation as pressure builds once again inside me. I arch my back, taking him in as far as I can, and he grunts as he thrusts faster against me. I grip the sheets into a fist, my breasts bouncing against the mattress as I match Liam's rhythm. I press my face into the mattress to muffle my loud moans and with a final thrust I lose all control, my body writhing against him as I come, savoring the release that floods through me.

Once our breathing slows, Liam moves to lie down next to me. I turn onto my side and prop myself up, looking into his eyes.

"Well, you certainly know how to wear a girl out." I grin, exhaling loudly. "I think three orgasms in one night might be my record."

"That was nothing." He smirks, wrapping an arm around me. "You should see me on a good day."

Did my stuck-up suit of a boss just make a joke?

I laugh, rolling over to rest my head on his hard chest.

My lips are swollen from kissing him, and I can tell Liam is just as spent as I am. I close my eyes, ready to sink into the reverie of the night. I smile as I drift off, thinking there's nowhere I'd rather be.

I blink my eyes open, disoriented for a second at the sunlight. I'm turned to the edge of the bed, staring out a huge floor to ceiling window at a beautiful garden with a gazebo in the middle. My heart skips a beat before the memory of where I am comes flooding back.

I turn over, but the other side of the California king bed is empty. I stretch out from beneath the white down comforter, sitting up. On the bedside table is a note written in Liam's small, neat handwriting.

Meet me in the kitchen, love.

Stacked next to the note is a t-shirt and pair of athletic shorts, along with a new toothbrush and tube of toothpaste. I almost laugh as I pull on the clothes and head to the bathroom to brush my teeth. Leave it to Liam to be so type A he has a day-after-sex starter kit.

I pad down the wooden staircase and into the kitchen, still in awe of his home. I walk across the marble tiled entryway and follow the smell of bacon to the kitchen, which is huge and stunning with granite countertops, every stainless steel appliance you could imagine and a long island with a breakfast bar. Liam is standing with his back to me, wearing a pair of dark jeans and a black t-shirt. I sneak up behind him and slip my arms around his waist, pressing myself into him. He turns from his cooking, smiling at me. Based on the clean, soapy smell of his skin it's clear he's already showered, and his hair is combed neatly into place. I almost want to laugh at how uptight he is, even in his own home.

But it's also kind of adorable.

"Good morning." I smile up at him as he spins around and pulls me against him, planting a gentle kiss on my lips.

"Did you sleep okay?" he asks as I move next to him to examine what he's cooking.

"I don't think I've ever slept so well," I admit, leaning against the counter. "Then again, I don't usually do so much strenuous activity right before bed."

He laughs, flipping the bacon, which sizzles in the pan.

"Can I help?" I ask.

"Do you want to make the eggs?" he asks, pointing toward the carton.

"Sure." I grab it and take a pan from the rack above the stove.

"I usually cook eggs in the smaller one," he says quickly, and I pause, raising an eyebrow. He lets out a small laugh. "Sorry. I'm a little set in my ways, I guess."

I grin, setting the pan down and turning on the stove.

"You? Rigid? I hadn't noticed," I say sarcastically, cracking an egg into the hot pan. "I assure you I make an amazing fried egg, so you can relax."

He smiles, pulling the bacon from the pan and setting it on two plates. He places two slices of bread in the toaster and sets the table with butter, jam and Nutella.

"You know the real way to a girl's heart." I grin at him, sliding the eggs onto the plates and bringing them to the table. "Bacon and Nutella."

"I do what I can." He smiles, and my stomach flips. I'm happy to see that he hasn't shaved yet, and the five o'clock shadow highlights his jawline and defined cheekbones. In the bright sunlight I notice flecks of gold in his green eyes as we chat over breakfast. I force myself not to stare, but I feel like I could look at him all day and never get tired of it.

Once we're finished eating I help him clear the

table and stretch out my arms.

"Well, I guess I should get going," I say, turning toward the bedroom. "I don't want to hijack your whole day."

"Oh." There's disappointment in his voice. "I was thinking you could stay," he says, his face falling for a moment. "If you don't have anything else to do, that is."

I grin, my heart jumping up into my throat. Usually after my first night with someone it's so awkward that I can't wait to leave, but there's something so sweet about the fact that Liam wants me to stay. I figured he'd wake up rigid, saying he needed to work or something, but I love this version instead.

"There's a great farmer's market around here, or we could catch a matinee, get an early dinner," he trails off, a devilish grin creeping across his face. "Maybe do some more of that strenuous activity."

I laugh, walking over to him and sliding my arms around his waist.

"I think I can move some things around in my schedule to make that work."

He leans down to kiss me, but before our lips

touch I hear the sounds of a key in the lock.

"Who…" he starts and trails off as we hear a small voice shout, "Daddy!"

I watch as what seemed like a dream come true turns into my worst nightmare. Liam's three kids just burst through the door, trailed by a woman I can only assume is his ex-wife. She's tall and thin, with long, red hair that's styled perfectly straight. She's wearing a tight blouse, black jeans, heels and Jackie O sunglasses. She looks so glamourous that I instantly feel like something that crawled out of the dumpster fire in my baggy clothes and un-brushed sex hair.

"Liam, I need you to… Oh," she says, stopping in her tracks as she sees me. Her eyes move up and down my body, taking in the fact that I'm wearing Liam's clothes.

Shit!

I feel a flush creep into my cheeks as I real-ize it's painfully obvious what happened between Liam and I last night.

The kids run up to give Liam hugs, and he picks Charlie up as the girls cling to his legs.

"Hey kiddos," he says, grinning at them. "I

didn't think I'd see you until next week."

"I need you to watch them today," his ex says coldly, tearing her eyes away from me to look at Liam. "That is, if you're not already doing something else." She glances back at me, putting an emphasis on the word *doing*. I try my best to appear unbothered, even though I feel like bolting back to my apartment to hide under the covers. Liam sets Charlie down with a pat on the head.

"You can't just come barging in here like this," he says in a low voice to her as the kids run into the playroom off the kitchen. "This isn't your house anymore."

"And whose fault is that?" she snaps at him, before closing her eyes and putting her hands up. "I don't have time for this. I cut my finger making breakfast and I need stitches."

She holds out a hand, her finger wrapped in a bloody bandage.

"Jesus, Lexi, that looks bad. Are you alright?" Liam asks, his tone instantly softening as he takes a step toward her to examine the cut.

She pulls her hand away, stepping back from him.

"It's fine. I don't need you to look at it, I need a doctor. Can you just watch the kids today?"

He nods. "Of course, don't worry about it."

She walks into the playroom to hug the kids goodbye before passing back through the kitchen. As she walks by she gives me a look so cold it could shatter glass, and I have to hold back a gasp. I've never been so obviously hated by someone I don't even know before, and I'm clearly not well equipped for it. She turns to give Liam a similar look before walking out the front door without another word.

I watch her with my jaw hanging open, shocked that Liam was able to spend an hour with her, never mind marry her and produce three children. She's like every super villain rolled into one deceptively beautiful woman. I'm finally understanding the horrific divorce he alluded to, and all the complications that came with it.

"Give me a second." He turns to me, gripping my arms with his hands and giving me a quick kiss on the forehead. He heads into the playroom where the kids are racing toy cars.

"Who wants to watch a movie?" he asks and the kids jump up, screaming, "Me, me, me."

They trail behind him as he shepherds them toward the stairs. Charlie pauses before walking down and turns to me.

"Who are you?" he asks sweetly.

"I'm Noelle. I'm a friend of your dad's," I say, smiling down at him.

"Why are you wearing his clothes?" he asks.

I open my mouth, not sure how to proceed, when Liam swoops in and saves me.

"Charlie, let's give Noelle a break before we start interrogating her," he says, patting Charlie on the head. "You better get upstairs before your sisters pick out the movie without you."

Charlie glances at me once more before bolting up the steps. Liam shakes his head, grinning at me, and I stifle a laugh.

Once they're gone I sneak up the stairs, gathering up my clothes and purse. Just when I've finished strapping on my heels Liam walks into the room.

"Sorry about Lexi," he says, sighing. "Sometimes she can be…"

"Terrifying?" I offer, and he laughs.

"Yes, exactly," he says, brushing a strand of hair behind my ear. "I feel terrible that our day is ruined."

I wave a hand in the air. "Totally not ruined," I say, shaking my head and smiling. "I knew you a had a lot going on when I agreed to this. And between running a company, raising three kids and dealing with a divorce, I'd be more weirded out if things *didn't* get crazy sometimes."

"I know I come with a lot of baggage, but please don't let it scare you off." His voice is gentle, his green eyes latching intently onto mine. "I had an amazing time last night."

I swallow, and cup his jaw with my hand.

"I did, too." I stand on my tiptoes to give him a quick kiss. "Go be a dad today. We'll talk tomorrow at work."

He nods, then walks me down the stairs. He insists on ordering my Uber, and I'm blown away by how sweet he is. Seeing him with his kids is a whole other side of him I didn't know existed. Between our date last night, the mind-blowing sex and seeing him with his family, I'm starting to think I could get used to being a part of Liam Bennett's life.

CHAPTER EIGHT

Liam

"**F**irst we'll pitch the structural changes and then we'll pull out our dildos and use them on each other's butts. Sound good, buddy?"

"Hmm?" I raise my head at Jamie's voice, his words not quite registering.

He scoffs, annoyed with me. "What the hell is with you today? You have the attention span of a gnat and you obviously haven't been listening to a word I've said." His brows are creased, and his concerned gaze is locked on mine.

"I was listening," I lie.

We've been meeting in my office for the past twenty minutes, discussing a new building project,

I think. Shit, actually I'm not sure. I think we may have finished that discussion a few minutes ago. I have no idea what topic we're on now.

He grins. "So you heard the part where I offered to peg you with a pink dildo?"

I break into easy laughter. "Okay you got me, I wasn't listening. And you're not getting anywhere near my arse. Sorry, mate."

"So, tell me what's wrong then. What's got you so wound up this time?" Jamie crosses one long leg over the other, leaning back in his chair and waiting for me to come clean. Even if I wanted to keep my little office tryst with Noelle a secret, not much gets by Jamie. And besides, he's my best friend, it wouldn't hurt to hear his perspective on things.

"Nothing's wrong. I'm just distracted is all." I lean closer, placing my elbows on the desk between us. "I may have started seeing someone. It's new."

Jamie's features soften. He had a front row seat to the collapse of my marriage, and all the anguish I went through when I learned that Lexi was cheating. And he's watched in silent protest as I remained single throughout my entire lengthy separation. "Fuck yeah, that's great man. It's about damn time."

He might not think it's so great if he knew I was shagging my assistant.

"Who's the lucky lady?" he asks, reading my mind.

I smirk, trying to hide my discomfort. "Noelle St. James." *God, even her name is cute.*

Jamie's brows pinch together in surprise. "Your assistant?"

"The very one."

His mouth twitches. "But that's so unlike you."

I grin. "I know." And there's something about that fact that feels remarkably good. Like I was shedding my skin and emerging on the other side of this mess a new man. Someone who remembered that sometimes you had to take a risk in order to enjoy a big payoff. It felt bloody fantastic.

"You sure you know what you're doing?"

I run one hand through the hair at the back of my neck. "Not a fucking clue. But I'm having fun doing it."

Fun doesn't even begin to describe it.

The memory of Noelle in my bed?

I can't let my mind go there or I'll spring a sudden erection in front of Jamie.

He nods. "Then that's all that matters. You're smart. You'll figure it out."

I sure as hell hope so.

"And if it goes to shit, you can always find a new assistant." At that, he rises and nods once before strolling from the office.

Watching the door slide closed, I frown. That thought hadn't occurred to me. If this goes well, and Noelle and I end up dating, she can no longer be my assistant. Barking out orders at your assistant is one thing—doing it to your girlfriend is quite another. And if it ends badly and we break things off, she'd certainly want to leave for a job where she didn't have to see her ex-fling every day.

But Jamie's right, I can't worry about all that just yet. For once in my life, I'm going to do something that's just for me. Instead of fulfilling an obligation, I'm going to fulfill a fantasy. And sexy, sweet, funny Noelle is the perfect person for the job.

"You can't be serious. That movie is so bad." Noelle shakes her head.

I groan with mock disgust. "It's a classic. I watch it every year on Christmas Eve."

Noelle chuckles and rolls her eyes, clearly not agreeing that *Die Hard* is one of the best Christmas films of all time.

When I'd asked her to come here for dinner tonight, it'd really been selfish on my part. I loved the idea of being alone here together with no distractions, and no one to share her with.

And it had nothing at all to do with the fact that my bed was a mere fifty paces away.

Nothing at all.

Yeah right.

But God, she makes me feel like a teenager again. She has the unique ability to level me with one flirty stare, one cheeky remark, and I'm done.

Which was why I found myself half-hard during dinner. I rarely have time to cook, but I do enjoy it. And tonight I'd made her one of my favorite dishes—risotto with mushrooms and goat cheese, a simple salad on the side and crisp white wine. The adoring look in her eyes as I plated her food and brought it to her could have reduced me to a puddle on the floor.

And now, we're seated side by side on the couch, discussing favorite movies—hers are chick flicks, and hobbies—she likes pottery and yoga, and a multitude of other things, I'm learning.

Noelle swirls her wine, finishing the last sip before setting the glass on the coffee table.

"Did you bring your swimsuit like I asked?"

She nods, her gaze landing on mine. "It's in my purse. Why? What did you have in mind?"

My voice drops lower. "Go change and I'll show you."

I point her toward my bedroom at the end of the hall, and Noelle disappears inside.

By the time I've changed into a pair of navy swim trunks in the guest bathroom, Noelle emerges from my room dressed in a tiny white two-piece bikini with little pineapples printed all over it in a happy pattern.

I almost swallow my damn tongue. Her curves are exquisite, and I want to fill my hands with them *immediately*. Instead I work to keep my eyes on hers.

Noelle does no such thing. Her gaze tracks hotly down my torso, her pulse thrumming wildly in her throat as she takes me in. I feel like a piece of prized meat being appraised by the butcher. I almost puff out my chest with pride. *Almost.*

It makes me glad for all the extra hours I spent at the gym trying to avoid dealing with the shit in my personal life.

"This way," I say, mouth twitching, once she's had her fill.

Noelle blinks once, her teeth dragging against her lower lip in a way that is so enticing.

When I open the glass door to my backyard, the chill in the air nips at our skin, but it's only a few short steps along the travertine walkway until we reach the warm, bubbling water of my hot tub.

"Oh wow. This is magical back here," she says.

It really is. There's a cedar arbor perched high above the jetted spa tub, with a lovely globe chandelier hanging from the center.

Noelle doesn't wait for an invitation. She steps into the water, sighing softly as she sinks down. The tops of her breasts are barely visible above the water, but it doesn't stop my libido from roaring to life.

"So what else do you like to do for fun?" I ask, settling beside her.

My life in comparison to hers is quite boring. Between work and my kids, there's little downtime that's just for me. And even if there were, I wouldn't have the first clue how to fill it.

But I like listening to Noelle talk, and I'm enjoying learning more about the woman who's kept me operating at such efficiency at work for the past three months.

She closes her eyes briefly, considering my question as the water swirls around us.

"There's nothing I won't try once. You name it, I've probably done it. Swing dancing. Salsa lessons. Sky diving. I even got into long distance running before I hurt my foot and had to give it up."

I nod, chuckling at her. "You're quite adventurous," I say, reaching up to tuck a loose strand of hair behind her ear.

Noelle meets my eyes, and it's then that I wonder if I'm one of the things she's trying on for size—a fun distraction from the day to day grind. *Fuck, I hope not.*

Rather than dwell on it, I push the somber thought from my head. Tonight isn't supposed to be filled with worry about the future. Tonight is supposed to be fun. Me embracing my life in a way that I nearly forgot how to do.

Noelle moves closer on the bench seat until her thigh grazes mine, and my heart begins pumping faster, all my doubts slipping away.

"Tonight has been amazing," she says, eyes on mine.

I bring my lips to hers for a soft kiss. "I quite agree."

I couldn't seem to stop touching her. Affection-ately running my fingertips along her spine, gently caressing her palm as I held her hand in mine. I didn't realize I was so starved for affection until Noelle.

"I liked watching you in the kitchen," she ad-mits, voice now soft.

By the time her hand drifts under the water, I'm so hard my cock aches for her attention. I wasn't going to be the one to tell her that, however. I'd invited her here for dinner because I enjoyed her company and wanted to spend more time with her. And I'd wanted to make it up to her since we'd had our last date interrupted. I wanted to watch her face light up in laughter and see her let her walls down. And just because I fed her, I don't expect anything physical to happen.

Only now, it was clear that she wanted it to. The lust-filled look in her honey-colored eyes and the way she wets her lower lip with the tip of her tongue are clear indicators.

Her silky palm drifts over my thigh, moving closer to her target. My pulse quickens as I let her hand explore.

She cups me gently, squeezing my shaft and slowly stroking me through the thin fabric of my wet bathing trunks. It feels fucking wonderful.

Her eager hands work on the tie holding my trunks together, and then she's running her palm up my shaft in one smooth motion.

A groan rumbles inside my chest, and I take her jaw in my hands, guiding her mouth to mine.

Kissing Noelle is a thing of beauty. Her full lips part, and her greedy tongue sucks on mine.

I make quick work of her bikini top, tugging on the strings holding it in place, and then fill my hands with the soft weight of her beautiful breasts.

Lightly teasing her, I graze my thumbs over her nipples, and she trembles and leans into my touch.

If I'd been worried before about her backing off over my personal-life drama, all thoughts of that have disappeared.

Her mouth moves to my neck while her hand continues its naughty magic below the water.

"Love?" I groan, my tone deep and husky. "Maybe we should go to my bedroom." I don't particularly want to come in my hot tub. I want to come inside Noelle—preferably after I've wrung one or two orgasms from her eager body.

She chuckles, teasing me. "But we just got in."

"Yes, and I clearly overestimated my self-control when you're near."

The cheeky little mix grins at me. "You have a thing for pineapples, huh?"

My gaze drifts down to the front of her chest where her bikini top is still askew. "I have a thing for *your* pineapples," I clarify.

"Yeah?" she breaths.

Somehow I know that when I get to work in the morning there will be a fucking pineapple sitting on my desk. I smile at the thought.

"Let's go inside," I suggest, and she nods, her half-lidded eyes colliding with mine.

When we rise to our feet and exit the water, I wrap her body in a fluffy white towel, tying another around my waist. Then we head inside, leaving wet footprints along the wood floors as we make our way down the hall.

I don't bother with the light, the room is dimly lit with a soft-glowing lamp in the corner from when she changed earlier.

While she shimmies out of her damp bathing suit, I unknot the towel from my waist and drop it to the floor.

I offer her my hand, and Noelle accepts, stepping closer until I can gather her into my arms and kiss the delicate column of her throat.

When I pull back and meet her eyes, she smiles shyly at me.

"What is it?" She's never been shy before, and I'm genuinely curious.

"You have a really nice dick."

I swallow, trying to hide my amusement. "Is

that so?"

I can't say my dick has ever been called *nice* before. The American girls I dated in the past generally seemed surprised I was uncut, but otherwise offered no complaints.

We move to the bed and roll toward the center together.

Having Noelle here in my bed, where I can see her stretched out against my pillows, makes me smile. It's in this bed where I've laid awake so many nights feeling alone and lonely. But not tonight. Tonight, I have a beautiful woman in my arms. A woman who makes me feel like I could accomplish anything.

"What?" she asks, her mouth lifting in an amused grin.

She's perfect, but the words lodge in my throat. I can't tell her that. My head is telling me to keep this casual, even if my heart is already getting other ideas.

"Are you cold?" I ask instead.

Noelle shakes her head. "Come here."

I move over her, and all this skin-to-skin contact makes me impossibly harder.

My cock slides against her soft pussy and I fight back a groan.

"Liam," she breathes.

"Yes, love?" I lean down to capture one perky nipple in my mouth, teasing it with my tongue.

She whimpers, thrusting her hips up to get more contact. "I want you," she murmurs.

After repeating the same treatment to her other breast, Noelle is practically shaking with need. Reaching between us, she grips my length again, and sends a curse rumbling in my throat.

"Condom," she groans.

I reach for the drawer in the table beside my bed and make quick work of sheathing myself in the latex. Then I move back over on top of her and kiss her lips, her neck, her collarbone while my hips grind slowly over hers, rubbing my erection over the slick flesh between her thighs.

Noelle groans again, her fingernails biting into my skin where she grips me—on my biceps, my back—anywhere she can reach.

"You want my cock, sweetheart?"

"So much." She angles her hips up to meet me,

rubbing her hot, smooth pussy all over my shaft.

I growl out a curse. Teasing her was fun, but she's right. I can't fucking wait any longer either. Aligning myself with her warm center, I give one long, slow thrust until I'm buried inside my own personal version of heaven.

Once I get inside Noelle, all the stress of my week vanishes in an instant.. It's crazy, but she just has that effect on me. She's so tight and so sexy and she's making the most wonderful pleasure-filled whimpers.

Moving above her, I press a soft kiss to her parted lips.

She tucks her knees in firmly against my ribs, squeezing me with her inner muscles.

Fuck.

That feels incredible.

I draw back, easing almost all the way out before her hands capture my ass, forcing me back where she wants me.

"You feel so good," she moans.

There's something so intimate about the way her arms hold me close, and the needy way our mouths find each other's. I keep waiting for this to feel strange—being with my assistant this way—but there are no thoughts of that. We fit together perfectly.

I need to go slow and pace myself or she's going to finish me, and I'm not anywhere near ready for this to be over.

Changing our positions, I withdraw, and pull her on top of me until she's straddling my thighs.

"Ride me, baby," I encourage, my hands stationed on the soft swell of her hips.

She rises up on her knees, aligning herself perfectly before sinking down so slowly that we both let out a slow hiss.

Noelle's lips part and she sucks in a shaky inhale. Then she puts her hands on my chest and begins to move in short, purposeful strokes designed to make me lose my damn mind.

"Fuck," I pant.

Noelle's beautiful tits bounce as she moves, and my body responds to the sight, everything within me tightening at once, like a coil ready to snap.

"Oh Liam," she moans, long and low. "You're going to make me…"

"Yes, love. That's it," I encourage.

Gripping her ass in both hands, I push my hips up, rocking into her more firmly.

One more deep thrust and Noelle shudders and clenches around me. Her rhythm falters as her tight heat grips me, milking me, and then I'm done for—coming in thick spurts as I pull her down toward my chest so I can take her lips while I empty myself into the condom.

The sound of her breathing my name pulses through me—and some unnamed emotion flares inside me—filling all the empty spaces left behind.

Tugging her into my arms, I roll us onto our sides. Chest still rising in quick inhalations, Noelle's eyes meet mine, and damn ... this woman. I don't see how I'll ever get enough of her.

With a soft sigh, she presses her cheek to my chest. "That was ..."

"Fuck yeah it was," I say, still breathless.

Noelle giggles.

So much for the articulate CEO, but being with her makes me feel like the version of myself I'd been missing all these years. The guy who knew how to leave work at work, and who remembered how to have fun. If I've learned anything over the past few years, it's that life is too short, and there are no guarantees.

But there are second chances, and maybe No-elle is mine.

CHAPTER NINE

Noelle

"How did you not die?" Jess asks, her mouth hanging open.

I had just relayed the story of my nightmare run in with Liam's ex and kids over dinner with Jess and Maxine. I haven't seen them in a while, and I have a lot to catch them up on.

"So, other than the dragon lady, operation bang your boss is going well?" Maxine asks as she swallows a mouthful of pasta. "I can't believe it took you so long to have sex with him."

I laugh, taking a sip of my wine. "I was trying not to lose my job, remember?" I say, shaking my head at her with a grin. "And you can stop calling it operation bang my boss."

"How is he in bed?" Jess asks eagerly, leaning forward.

"Unbelievable," I tell them. I've had a permanent grin on my face ever since I started seeing Liam, and I've been dying to tell someone about it. All the secrecy at work was fun at first, but I'm ready to be more open about my feelings for him. And my feelings have grown from more than just physical. I like him. Maybe more than I should. But he's one of the good guys, and even if this started off as just a crush, my heart didn't get that memo.

"And you thought sleeping with him was a bad idea," Maxine says, shaking her head in mock disappointment. "I hate to say I told you so…"

"Okay, you guys were right," I say, holding up my hands. "And who knew I'd actually end up liking him?"

"Like him?" Jess asks, her tone low and concerned. "As in, you have feelings for him?"

I pause, confused by the sudden change. "Yeah, I have feelings for him." *How could I not?* "What's wrong with that?"

"When you said you guys were going on that date a couple weeks ago, we assumed it was a Netflix and chill situation," Maxine says, watching me over the rim of her drink.

"No, not that kind of date. It was a real date, in public, with clothes on," I tell them slowly, suddenly on edge.

Jess and Maxine exchange a look.

"I thought this was just a sex thing," Maxine says, clearly disappointed in me.

"We like each other. Last time I checked, that was a good thing." I raise an eyebrow, still trying to wrap my head around the fact that they aren't as excited as I am about this.

"It is a good thing," Jess says quickly, elbowing Maxine. "You should explore all of your options."

"But doesn't he have three kids? And isn't he technically still married?" Maxine asks, ignoring Jess's elbow.

"Well, yes," I say slowly, my heart sinking. I thought my friends would be happy for me, but suddenly I feel like I've done something very wrong. "His divorce isn't final yet, but you guys were the ones who wanted me to do this, and now that I have it's bad? What's going on?"

"Nothing," Jess says in a calm voice, clearly trying to diffuse the situation. "It just sounds so…

complicated."

"It's one thing to have sex with the British hottie, but to actually be in a relationship… with a single dad," Maxine trails off, finishing her glass of cabernet. "Trust me, you don't want to let feelings get involved. It'll ruin all the fun."

I laugh them off with a wave of my hands. "You worry too much. Seriously, it's not that complicated. So he's got a past, who doesn't?"

I finish my plate of penne, refusing to let their pessimism ruin my excitement about Liam. If they met him, they'd understand. Yes, he's my boss, but he's also one of the sweetest, most considerate men I've ever been with. Seeing him open up around his kids only made me want to know him more. My friends might think they have my best interests at heart, but they're wrong. The situation with Liam isn't too messy, or a mistake. In fact, I've never felt so sure about anything in my life.

I flip through the latest issue of *Cosmopolitan* and skim an article titled "Sexy Ways to Surprise Your Man." Although the idea of walking up to Liam and handing him my panties in the middle of the workday sounds fun, I'm not sure if that's the kind of surprise I'm looking for.

It's been a month since my disaster dinner with Jess and Maxine, where they'd tried to tell me my relationship with Liam was doomed to fail. Far from it, we're better than ever, spending every spare second we can together. The only problem is that Liam's been under a crazy amount of stress trying to lock down a huge deal for the company so he can pay his divorce settlement. If he doesn't land the deal, he'll have to sell the company he's worked a decade for to come up with the money to pay off Lexi. It's a scary thing, because there is a rival investment firm that's been hinting at wanting to acquire Griffin. If they do, Liam will have to step down as CEO and I'm sure several of us would be out of a job.

I've been trying to think of something special to do for him to take the edge off, but I'm having a hard time coming up with ideas. I thought of getting us a nice hotel room for a staycation, but my bank account is in such a sorry state that the nicest hotel I can afford is the Motel 6 by the airport. A cheap continental breakfast and the sound of airplanes keeping us up all night isn't exactly the kind of soothing romantic getaway I was envisioning.

Still, I'm hoping with a little creativity I can still surprise him with something special. After an afternoon of brainstorming, I decide to invite Liam over to my place for a night of pampering. We almost never hang out here, which is mostly because of me. My shoe box of an apartment doesn't exactly live up to his giant, sun-filled mansion.

When he arrives, I'm just pulling dinner out of the oven. I give him a quick kiss, my heart fluttering when he moves a hand to the small of my back to press me in closer. Even though we've been seeing each other for over a month, I still get butterflies around him. He looks irresistible in a casual button up flannel and dark jeans. He's definitely learned to relax around me since we first started dating, and he even left his hair tousled the way I like it.

He sniffs at the air once I've gotten him seated in the living room with a glass of wine.

"It smells amazing," he says, smiling. "What did you make?"

"It's a surprise," I tell him with a grin. "Follow me into the kitchen."

I've set my small table with candles and my only two matching plates. It's not a five-star restaurant, but it's as romantic as a girl on a budget can get.

"You did all this?" he asks, pulling me in for another kiss.

"This is nothing," I say with a wink. "Just wait for the rest of the night."

I put his plate down and he looks up incredulously.

"You made this?"

"It's your favorite from childhood, right?" I ask, hoping I didn't totally get this wrong. "Shepherd's pie?"

"Yeah, but how did you—"

"You mentioned it once." I shrug as a grin creeps across his face. "It was a while ago, but I remembered and thought it would be a nice surprise."

"I can't believe you did that for me," he says, his green eyes locking with mine. "It's so sweet of you to remember that."

I raise my glass of wine to toast. "I know you're been under a lot of pressure, so tonight is your night to relax and be pampered." I grin. "Cheers."

We clink glasses and Liam dives into the food. I can't help but laugh.

"I don't think I've ever seen you attack your food before."

"This is amazing. Seriously, Noelle, never tell my mum, but this is better than hers."

"Don't thank me yet. Your night of relaxation is only beginning," I say coyly.

Once we've finished dinner I leave Liam in the kitchen with another glass of wine while I set up the next part of his surprise. After a few minutes I beckon for him to follow me to the bedroom, where I've turned the lights off and filled every available surface with soy candles. I also set up my diffuser to blow calming essential oils into the room. It's the closest my tiny one-bedroom apartment will ever come to being a spa.

"Welcome to your personal massage room," I say, as he looks at me with his mouth pulled into a questioning smirk.

"This looks so good." He glances around the room, before turning to kiss me on the forehead.

"How do you like your massages? Soft or rough?" I ask, smirking. "Oh, and clothes off, please."

"I think you know I like it rough." He winks, pulling off his shirt and jeans and climbing into the bed.

"Put this on," I instruct, handing him an eye mask.

"Are you about to go *Fifty Shades of Grey* on me?" he asks, taking the mask from me with a raised eyebrow.

"Are you always this difficult when you go to the spa?" I ask sarcastically. "Don't worry, the mask is just to help you relax."

He slips it on and when I'm sure he can't see me I strip off my clothes quietly. I turn on calming ocean sounds, then grab a bottle of essential oil and climb onto the bed. He's lying face down, and I straddle his hips, pouring the warm massage oil on him. When I start rubbing his shoulders, he groans.

"Noelle, this is amazing," he sighs. "I can't believe you went to all this trouble."

"Shh," I tell him, massaging his scalp. "Just relax and enjoy."

I keep rubbing his shoulder blades, which are tense and full of knots. I work him over, moving down his spine and back up. Once I'm sure he's sufficiently relaxed, I ease up, my fingertips becoming lighter, more sensual in their touches.

After a while, I lean forward so that my breasts

graze his back, and I feel him stir beneath me. He lifts up his eye mask and turns back, taking in the fact that I'm not wearing any clothes.

"Jesus," he breathes. "Do you do naked massages for all your clients?" he asks playfully.

I laugh. "Only the really sexy ones."

I try to keep rubbing his neck, but he stops me.

"I can't wait any longer to touch you," he says in a low voice, turning over. His body is such a work of art, and I can't help taking in his hard biceps and sculpted abs, finally resting my eyes between his legs at his quickly growing erection.

He reaches a hand up to brush a strand of hair behind my ear, then cups my face in his hands.

"Thank you for being so sweet and thoughtful," he says, and my heart beats faster against my chest. I bend down to kiss him gently on the lips, running my hands through his hair.

"You're amazing," he whispers as I pull back.

"You're not so bad, either," I say, smiling down at him. I feel his erection pressing into me, and I bite my lip.

"I think I missed a spot," I say quietly, reaching

a hand down to stroke him. He groans and closes his eyes as I cup his balls in my hand. I bend over, my mouth exploring his neck and chest as I continue to stroke his length. I feel him growing harder in my hand as I kiss a line down his abs, running my tongue along his stomach toward his eager erection. I put my mouth over the tip of him, savoring the sound of his sharp inhale. I move my mouth further down, taking more of him until his full length is in my mouth.

"That feels so good," he grunts.

I continue to move slowly, wanting to draw out his pleasure. He reaches down a hand to grip my hair and I move faster, my breathing coming in sharply through my nose. Before he can finish, I climb on top of him, rubbing myself against him so he can feel how wet I am. He tilts my chin up so I'm looking into his green eyes.

"Fuck me, sweetheart," he murmurs.

Raising up just a bit on my knees, I use my hand to guide him between my thighs. We had *the talk* a few days ago about our sexual pasts, and decided to forgo condoms since I'm on birth control, but this is the first time we've actually done the deed.

I sink down slowly, allowing my body to accommodate the stretch, and Liam's eyes fall closed.

"Holy fuck," he groans, a deep rumble in his chest.

As I lean down to press my lips to his, Liam takes control, thrusting his hips up in time with the steady rhythm of my heartbeat.

Pleasure whips through me and I can't help but whimper. He feels amazing.

I've never felt so comfortable with someone so quickly before, and being with Liam is unlike any other relationship I've had. He might have a complicated life, but the connection between us is simple.

I never thought I'd say it, but I'm falling for Liam Bennett, and fast. And yeah there are probably a million details to figure out like our working arrangement and if I'm really cut out to be a stepmom, but right now, I refuse to let my friends be right. This right here, being in this man's arms is the only thing that matters.

CHAPTER TEN

Liam

"**D**id you finish preparing those documents?" I ask Jeff, my new assistant. He looks up eagerly, handing over a stack of files I asked him to work this morning.

It's been a little over six months since Noelle and I started dating, and things have been pretty damn amazing. Noelle was recently promoted to a leadership role in a new department, so I'm no longer her direct boss. I hated letting go of the best assistant I've ever had, but Noelle's too talented to keep working in an entry level position. Besides, it's a lot easier to focus on work when I don't have a constant view of her backside.

Meanwhile, I was able to land the huge deal that allowed me to pay my divorce settlement. After a long, grueling process, everything is final, which means Noelle and I can finally be open about our relationship both inside and outside of work.

"I'm heading out soon, so I'll see you tomorrow," I tell Jeff, who nods and returns to work.

I stretch and sit back down at my desk. I still have a few things to finish up, and I'm engrossed in reading over a contract when I hear a faint knock at the door.

"Excuse me? Mr. CEO? Do you have a minute?"

I look up, grinning, as Noelle saunters into my office. My cock twitches as she walks over to me, heels clicking against the wood floor. Even after all this time, the sight of her in a skirt and heels still gets me going. She perches on the edge of my desk, and I can't help but think of the first time she did that, a little over six months ago, right before we shared our first kiss.

"How's the new assistant?" she asks, gesturing toward the desk outside my office.

"He's good. Seems like a hard worker. But he's nothing compared to my old one," I say with a wink, standing up to give her a quick kiss.

"Well, it's hard to beat an assistant who also wants to give you blow jobs." She smirks and I let out a chuckle.

"Shall we?" I ask, shutting my computer and gesturing toward the door. Ever since I started dating Noelle, I've been cutting down my hundred-hour work weeks and focusing on enjoying all the money I've made. The old me would never have left the office before eight, but the thought of spending time with Noelle is pretty good motivation for getting out the door on time. Plus, she's a huge supporter of me spending more time with my kids. They've gotten to know Noelle over these past few months, and it's obvious how much they like having her around.

As we walk the few blocks to a nearby bar, I slip a hand into Noelle's. It's a warm spring day, and the sunshine brings out the bright flecks in her eyes. Every time she looks up at me with those honey colored eyes, my heart pumps faster. Sometimes, I still can't believe how it all worked out. It's almost unreal that Noelle is mine.

We step into the dimly-lit bar and I have to blink a few times before I spot Jamie in the corner. Noelle's friends are next to him at the table, and they've clearly started the fun without us. Noelle and I have spent time with each other's friends separately, but we wanted them to finally meet. And from the looks of it, they've wasted no time getting to know each other.

"I hope Jamie isn't hitting on them," I sigh as we walk across the bar. The last thing I need is to have to diffuse a situation between him and Noelle's friends. We watch as Maxine laughs at something he says and tosses her long blonde hair over one shoulder.

"Trust me, my friends aren't the ones you need to be worried about," Noelle grins and I chuckle again.

"Ladies, is this degenerate bothering you?" I ask as we walk up, clapping Jamie on the back.

"Liam, you never told me you had such hot friends," Maxine says, winking at Jamie. "We need to hang out more often."

Noelle smiles, sitting down next to her.

"Easy, tiger," she says, slinging an arm around Maxine's shoulder.

Noelle confessed to me that her friends had reservations about our relationship at the start. Far from being offended, I'm glad she has friends who watch out for her. And considering the circumstances, I understand why they would question my intentions. Luckily, after the four of us spent some time together they understood that what was happening between Noelle and I wasn't just an office fling; we have a real connection.

"Jamie was just about to tell us a story about Liam from college," Jess says after the server comes around to take our drink orders. "Something about blowing up a tractor?"

Noelle looks at me with a raised eyebrow as I sit down next to her.

"You blew up a tractor?" she asks. "You've never mentioned that before."

"It's not as bad as it sounds." I raise my hands up in mock defense. "And if I recall it was technically Jamie's fault."

The server soon delivers our drinks, and Noelle smiles and nudges me with her shoulder. I pull her against me and give her a quick kiss on the forehead. I'm not the kind of man who likes big displays of affection in public, but with Noelle I'm like a teenager again. Sometimes, I just can't keep my hands to myself.

"So you're the bad boy," Maxine says slyly,

nodding toward Jamie. "What other naughty things have you done?"

"Ignore her," Noelle says to Jamie, playfully slapping Maxine's shoulder.

"What about Noelle?" I ask with a grin, turning toward Jess and Maxine. "Did she ever blow anything up?"

Noelle, Jess and Maxine look between each other, grinning.

"They're not going to tell us, are they?" Jamie asks, looking at me over the rim of his beer.

"No, I don't think they are," I laugh, sipping my whiskey neat.

"It's girl code," Maxine says with a shrug. "Some things are sacred."

"Just consider yourself lucky that you locked her down," Jess smiles at me from across the table. "There's never a dull moment with Noelle around."

"Trust me, I know." I smile, sliding a hand around Noelle's hips. I lift the fabric of her blouse slightly so I can run my fingers along the skin of her lower back. She glances up at me with a questioning look, then after a beat, slides a hand onto my thigh under the table. My cock pulses as she as she moves her hand slowly up and down my leg. I swallow a large part of my drink, trying to focus on the conversation and not on the sudden ache in my groin.

"I have to use the restroom," Noelle says pointedly, giving me a sly look. Once she walks away, I stand up, leaving the group, and follow her. She's waiting outside the restrooms, and when I walk up she grabs my hand and pulls me into the women's.

Inside, I waste no time locking us in a stall, then push her up against the door. We kiss hungrily, our tongues dancing into each other's mouths. I run my fingers along her thighs, lifting her skirt slightly as I move closer to the warmth between her legs. I kiss her neck and collarbone, savoring the feeling of her pulse quickening beneath my mouth. She lets out a moan as I tug at the string of her panties, and wraps her leg around my waist, pressing herself against me. I groan as she collides against the straining ridge in my trousers.

I can't believe how much happier and lighter I feel now that I'm with Noelle. I barely recognize the jaded, overworked CEO I was just six months ago. I never thought I'd be the guy who says cliché things about his girlfriend, but every day with her is like a breath of fresh air. I can't imagine what I would do without her, and now that my divorce is final and everything is figured out at work, I never have to find out.

After a minute the door opens, and someone comes in to wash their hands. We immediately freeze, trying to stay as silent as possible. As the woman runs the hand dryer Noelle looks up at me, biting her lip. She looks so sexy I want to forget that we have an audience and keep touching her, but I hold back. As soon as we hear the door swing shut Noelle lets out a loud exhale, and we start laughing.

"How about we continue this when we get home," I say, giving her a final kiss on the forehead. "Let's go pay and get out of here."

"Whatever you say." Noelle adjusts her skirt so she's covered again, then grins at me. "You're the boss."

I laugh, putting an arm around her as we leave the restroom. "I might be the boss, but you're the one in charge of my heart, love."

Thank you for reading!

If you enjoyed *Bossy Brit*, turn the page for another book you might love:

PLAYING FOR KEEPS

I've never been so stupid in my entire life.

My teammate's incredibly sweet and gorgeous younger sister should have been off-limits, but my hockey stick didn't get that memo.

After our team won the championship, and plenty of alcohol, our flirting turned physical and I took her to bed.

Shame sent her running the next morning from our catastrophic mistake. She thinks I don't remember that night—but every detail is burned into my brain so deeply, I'll never forget. The feel of her in my arms, the soft whimpers of pleasure I coaxed from her perfect lips...

And now I've spent three months trying to get her out of my head. Which has been futile, because I'm starting to understand she's the only girl I'll ever want.

I have one shot to show her I can be exactly what she needs, but Elise won't be easily convinced.

That's okay, because I'm good under pressure,

and this time, I'm playing for keeps.

If you like cocky foul-mouthed hockey players—
this is the book for you! Sexy broken alpha male
Justin is willing to risk it all—even his heart for a
chance with his friend's sister.

Available now at all major retailers

About the Author

A *New York Times*, *Wall Street Journal*, and *USA TODAY* bestselling author of more than two dozen titles, Kendall Ryan has sold over two million books, and her books have been translated into several languages in countries around the world. Her books have also appeared on the *New York Times* and *USA TODAY* bestseller list more than three dozen times. Kendall has been featured in publications such as *USA TODAY*, *Newsweek*, and *In Touch Magazine*. She lives in Texas with her husband and two sons.

To be notified of new releases or sales, join Kendall's private Mailing List.

www.kendallryanbooks.com/newsletter

Get even more of the inside scoop when you join Kendall's private Facebook group, Kendall's Kinky Cuties:

www.facebook.com/groups/kendallskinkycuties

Follow Kendall

Website

www.kendallryanbooks.com

Facebook

www.facebook.com/kendallryanbooks

Twitter

www.twitter.com/kendallryan1

Instagram

www.instagram.com/kendallryan1

Newsletter

www.kendallryanbooks.com/newsletter

Other Books by Kendall Ryan

Unravel Me
Filthy Beautiful Lies Series
The Room Mate
The Play Mate
The House Mate
The Impact of You
Screwed
The Fix Up
Dirty Little Secret
xo, Zach
Baby Daddy
Tempting Little Tease
Bro Code
Love Machine
Flirting with Forever
Dear Jane
Finding Alexei
Boyfriend for Hire
The Two Week Arrangement
Seven Nights of Sin
Playing for Keeps
All the Way
Trying to Score

For a complete list of Kendall's books, visit:

www.kendallryanbooks.com/all-books/